3 4028 08688 1597
HARRIS COUNTY PUBLIC LIBRARY

Harris
Harris, Elizabeth
Mayhem : three lives of a
woman

DISCARD

$20.00
ocn930036628

First edition.

Advance Praise for *Mayhem*

"In *Mayhem* the pitiful truth of m[...] is told in spare, sometimes lyric, so[...] early 20th century Texas German fa[...] reader will recognize age-old prejudices underlie personal choices. Strengths and follies of *Mayhem*'s characters are sources of both comedy and terror. One cannot help but acknowledge, through the ironic vision, including fictions within fiction, of Elizabeth Harris's work, 'Yes, life is like that.'"

—Carolyn Osborn, author of *Where We Are Now*

"In Elizabeth Harris's exquisite new novel about a small Central Texas community in the early decades of the last century, mayhem is something more and something different than the sort of violence or turbulence that the word commonly denotes: it is—more subtly, and more originally—a condition of the characters' ordinary lives and familiar relations. *Mayhem: Three Lives of a Woman* is one of the most intimate, vivid, and textured literary evocations of a bygone time and place and woman's life that I have read, yet also one of the most mysterious. That's because Harris possesses a combination of craft and wisdom found only in the finest historical novelists: the craft to render the past luminously in imagination, and the wisdom to recognize that that past can only be imagined, never known. Gripping, haunting, elusive, *Mayhem* is an extraordinary achievement."

—Evan Carton, author of *Patriotic Treason:*
John Brown and the Soul of America

D0862399

"A great novel gives us Genesis, and so *Mayhem: Three Lives of a Woman* calls a world into being. We get not only the odor and crackle of rural Texas beginning a hundred years ago, but also the spirits of that time and place. We suffer with a rancher's wife, a woman catastrophically misunderstood. Violence proves inevitable — but then comes the real miracle. Elizabeth Harris summons up not one world but several, in rich and moving succession. It's as if redemption were sympathy: as if to peer deeply into anyone is to understand everyone. If this sounds less like a God and more like a great storyteller, well, that's what we've got. Harris squeezes palaver and tears from her Texas clay, even while making sure we see the gifted hands at work."

— John Domini, author of *A Tomb on the Periphery* and
other novels, as well as stories, criticism, and poetry.

"*Mayhem* is a wonder of a novel. A careful evocation of time and place, community and character, pitched in a voice rich with the lyric poetry of everyday speech, the novel seems not so much narrated as blown up by a breeze. It's not enough to claim that I believed every word of it; I *felt* every syllable. his archetypal tale of crime and punishment, so filled with tragedy and sympathy, is one of the most wildly *alive* novels I have ever read. Every sentence teems with truths both literal and metaphorical, and yet, for all its wisdom and profundity, it reaches us in the manner of a folk ballad, high and sweet and clear."

— Michael Parker, author of *All I Have in This
World* and *The Watery Part of the World*

"With an eye for both the beauty of nature and the brutality of humans reminiscent of E. Annie Proulx, Elizabeth Harris tells the riveting story of a vicious crime and one woman's subsequent fall from grace. Set in Central Texas in the first half of the 20th century, *Mayhem: Three Lives of a Woman* captures the quirks and intricacies of rural Texas culture. *Mayhem's* protagonist, Evelyn Gant, navigates the constraints placed on women, and her necessary obedience to her husband results in a momentary concession that ends life as she knows it. Like the fiction of Marilynne Robinson, everything in Harris's writing is deeply consequential; and her ability to convey both the natural and social worlds of Texas in the 1930s astounds. Extraordinary!"

— Mary Pauline Lowry, author of *Wildfire*

Also By Elizabeth Harris

The Ant Generator, short stories

MAYHEM:

THREE LIVES OF A WOMAN

BY ELIZABETH HARRIS

WINNER OF THE GIVAL PRESS NOVEL AWARD

ARLINGTON, VIRGINIA

Copyright © 2015 by Elizabeth Harris.

This is a work of fiction. Names, characters, businesses, places, events and incidents are either the products of the author's imagination or used in a fictitious manner. Any resemblance to actual persons, living or dead, or actual events is purely coincidental.

All rights reserved under International and Pan-American Copyright Conventions. Printed in the United States of America.

With the exception of brief quotations in the body of critical articles or reviews, no part of this book may be reproduced or transmitted in any form or by any means, graphic, electronic, or mechanical, including photocopying, recording, taping, or by any information storage or retrieval system, without the permission in writing from the publisher.

Published by Gival Press, an imprint of Gival Press, LLC.

For information please write:
Gival Press, LLC
P. O. Box 3812
Arlington, VA 22203
www.givalpress.com

First edition
ISBN: 978-1-940724-00-3
eISBN: 978-1-940724-01-0
Library of Congress Control Number: 2015942115

Cover art: © Lane Erickson | Dreamstime.com.
Photo of Elizabeth Harris by Warwick Wadlington.
Design by Ken Schellenberg.

for Warwick Wadlington

1

A young woman climbing out of an old Essex in a cloche hat and a flowered maroon rummage-sale dress in front of the Prince Carl County courthouse, that's what some observers will remember—and everything they knew about her at the time. Not her companion, except as part of what they knew, a gray-haired woman leaning back to the window to talk to the driver. Just, for a memory-snapshot of time and place, the young woman Evelyn Gant standing at the bottom of monumental granite steps, spoken of in the county as pink but really an under-color like raw liver, flecked over with black and gray and the sparkle of mica. Some of these imagined observers who live in Meusebach go, or pretend to go, about their business on the Square; others who have driven in from the country or over from Iron Rock in hopes of getting in at the Gant brothers' trial stare openly at the young woman, whom they know at least by sight or name. A fictional character as they themselves are characters, to them she is a person: descendent of old settlers, daughter of one landowning family, married, *surely not for long now*, to the son of another; and part of her fascination, escorted and left waiting in the lemony light of the October morning, is that she seems almost in custody, a defendant herself. In fact, she is only a witness and, being the wife of one of the defendants, a limited witness, but she is the trial's most intriguing spectacle, the origin of the crime, the modest, obedient, well regarded woman taken in adultery. People think of her in that phrase, out of its context except as it explains her being sheltered by Sister and Brother White of Iron Rock First Baptist, a charitable act permissible because no Baptists are parties to the trial. The Whites are presumed to have their own hopes for her.

When Brother White drives on in the dignified rectangular car and Sister White and Mrs. Gant begin to climb the courthouse steps, there must be other people on them but, seen by a woman coming out from the grain-dusty smell of a grocery store, the two seem like the only ones. Half-hidden there in the inset doorway, she lays two fingers over her open mouth at the realization of *her*, trudging up the courthouse steps—how slowly!—as well she might, and suddenly knows herself virtuous and safe in her own life. But Evelyn Gant's pace has been set by Sister White, a little breathless, "Got to slow down," and Evelyn has merely obliged, mind chill and solid, past thinking, or before it. She can only feel, say, the sun warming the back of her black hat, the knees levering her body up the blocks of stone, the bulge of a napkin-wrapped biscuit tucked into her pocket by Sister White as a midday meal. Unshaven shins emerge, one and the other from under the hem of her dress, and seeing them, seeing the ankle-rolled, ill-fitting hose, the scuffed brown shoes she has laced daily for weeks, she who was formerly fastidious can only register with a dull surprise, *Mine.*

Heavy brass-fitted glassed doors gleam for a moment as they are opened, the two figures disappear into the dark courthouse, and that's all most people in Prince Carl County will see of Evelyn Gant at the trial of her husband and his brother. Every morning that week she will arrive with her soft-faced escort and, once inside the courtroom, will separate from her to sit in the scarred witnesses' section. But arriving and sitting will be all she does. The accused Gant brothers, the injured rural neighbor, and Evelyn herself are so widely connected in the county that the prosecution will fail to empanel a jury and the trial will be moved. Several counties away, far fewer people will recognize any of the principals. But newspaper reporters from Austin and San Antonio, even Ft. Worth, will have been attracted by the nature and rarity of a crime whose mention makes men cross their legs. The kind of crime an angry person says he or she would like to commit against some particular man so much more often than anybody ever does it that, in the allegation of its having been done, language seems to have been released to become an actor in the world.

As it is in this story—an admission that could seem, without being, too obvious to be made.

2

Principal of my story: Evelyn Kunkle, born in 1909 in Prince Carl County; married to Lester Gant, Jr., in 1927; to be divorced from him in 1937. Her mother was a Schlegel, his a Heimsoth, and, around there, all those German surnames in those years could still stab a historical memory that bled immigrants. Disembarked in the salty breeze of a green nowhere amid the smells of leather satchels and mildewed, iconic copies of Herodotus and Thucydides; loaded onto the creak of ox-drawn wagons up from the coast for a terrible overtaking, to the clink of chains, of the first black men and women some of them had ever seen, walked there on thick soles barefoot from—how far was Alabama? And afterwards, the old-time questions, how men could think slavery was right, how much an enslaved laborer sold for, how much a landowner could make with how many hands on a first cotton crop, the questions themselves conditioned by habits of mind: principle, ambition, and the necessary attention to business.

The settings of Prince Carl County, its county seat of Meusebach, and its subsidiary town of Iron Rock, are fictive places, invented partly from a mashup of places in Central Texas. Its country of rising plains and riverine woods was already a violent area by the time black and white settlers arrived, and their traditions would later tell stories about this bend of a wooded creek or that divergence of roads approaching a town where a particular named human had breathed out a life. The names of certain roads call to mind unpunished murders. The Kunkle and Schlegel forebears of Evelyn Gant are thus imagined ploughing prairie and cutting down trees, beeswaxing floors and boiling *knoedeln* with rifle at hand against spear-throwing, arrow-shooting horsemen from the Comanche empire who raided and killed and tortured in reprisal for this gradual white conquest of Hueco and Lipan and Tonkawa territories they themselves had earlier conquered. When the white men's justice scrabbled for a hold but was still a day's ride to be fetched and another to be brought back, witnesses might meanwhile be intimidated or shot, so the victims of a crime, or their survivors, might punish suspects more immediately. The need for all that would seem to have been eliminated by the building of railroads and stringing of telegraph wires. And yet—as if the abolished distances of the past had either gone on instructing people in the tradition or had never had as much to do with it as the land had made it seem—insofar as improvements in law enforcement eliminated the need for those summary approximations of justice, they did so only in one understanding of the word *need*.

3

As suburban children in Ft. Worth in the 1950's, my sister and I—also fictional characters, one a version of the fictional author—were taken to visit elderly relatives in small cautious Texas towns. Everybody in those places knew who everybody was, and we knew only our own family, and I felt the discomfort of being known without knowing. Our visits accompanying our mother, only child of her own widowed mother, to the town founded partly by their ancestors were ceremonious, the three of us arriving hatted and gloved on the same train Bonnie Parker was said to have left on and probably would have if she'd ever lived there. As soon as we were settled in my grandmother's small slope-floored, mildew-smelling house, we were obliged by respect for our and her elders to visit a widowed maternal aunt, Mrs. Theriot, who had helped to rear her.

Called Auntie by our and another branch of her family, Mrs. Theriot had broken a hip and, in a large pink granite house that survived as the last private residence on the main street, was confined to bed for what remained of her life. This would prove to be nearly fifteen years. She was served by the same durable woman who had cooked and kept house for her for decades, a Negro—I use the term of the times—and the same unrelated, also Negro, man who had chauffeured her when she could still go out. But we were let into a just-polished hallway that smelled faintly like overripe bananas by a white woman whom our mother greeted politely and our grandmother ignored. An orphaned poor relation and a snob, our grandmother awarded everyone in Iron Rock the grade of cordiality she believed fitting.

When we had climbed the staircase far enough to glimpse down over a gleaming banister into the kitchen, she called down, "Hello, Robbie," to the cook, who came out into the hallway with a towel in her hands and called up, "Good morning, Ms. Mack, and is that Miss Lizzie and her girls?" and we said good morning to Robbie.

We were led into a high-ceilinged front bedroom with tall windows, where Auntie lay propped up against a dark headboard, her square, bristly, humorous old face surrounded by a white fluff of permanent wave. In a semi-circle of assorted chairs around her bed sat a selection of visitors: any of her five surviving children or their families; sidelong relatives such as we were; aged friends who could still get around; the pastor or fellow members of the First Baptist Church next door, founded by our common forebears; and almost any white person, doctor, banker, optician, hairdresser, who had been in to attend to her and been invited to sit awhile. She held court.

My sister and I were introduced as "Miss Lizzie's girls," and the white woman was directed to fetch us glasses of Dr. Pepper—"Oh, they don't need that," our mother said—which arrived on a cork-lined tray. This woman, to whom I will give a name, though in memory she has none, fetched other things, as Auntie Theriot directed her in words—"That letter with the photo of young C. W., Evelyn"—or a gesture toward the blue-rimmed white kidney basin on the nightstand.

Auntie Theriot dipped snuff and spat black discreetly, never mind that her Baptists forbade the use of tobacco. She also played the forbidden cards with her diminishing group of ancient friends and, in a deep suave voice, told stories about herself that evoke an old woman in a Katherine Porter story.

"When I was a girl, and I was," she said to us, "Becka Thigpen, I rode cross-cut instead of side-saddle and broke horses with my brothers. And those things were not done by young ladies, my dears." That she had always been a lady, and that we all knew exactly what that was, were taken for granted. (Now is a place to say that I didn't, and when somewhat later in my growing up I realized I did understand, the whole thing, I couldn't believe it.)

Rebecca Leonora Thigpen had married her father's junior business partner, rough Ed Theriot, who might not have been quite a gentleman if she hadn't, had produced seven children with him, and, in my grandmother's approving recall, *addressed him as Mr. Theriot to the end of his days.* She owned the drugstore, Thigpen and Theriot, where several of her sons and grandsons worked, and enjoyed a reputation for such exact Baptist faith that, within the limits imposed by habit and injury, she appeared to do and say what she liked. This impressed me, as no one else I knew did.

For instance, she told what was called *mixed company* about the visit of a want-witted Miss Somebody, who had boasted of drinking a whole pot of coffee before going to bed and sleeping the night through: "If she did, I'll bet she peed the bed."

The mouth of my grandmother hung open in a small, dark oval. During a short interval later, when we had left the bedroom, she would say, *Auntie's old,* in an explanation that started out to be of the snuff and the playing cards fanned out on a bed-tray, although my sister and I, who were not being brought up Baptists, didn't understand what was supposed to be wrong about those things.

What I wanted to know was who, or what, that woman who waited on Auntie was. I had no experience with servants, let alone different levels of them, and this attendant seemed like the kind of woman we were required to call "Miss" or "Mrs." She wore, not a housedress like Robbie, but a dark, flower-sprigged rayon dress such as my grandmother wore to go visiting, with cloudy nylon stockings and stout, laced-up, chunk-heeled shoes.

When not fetching something, she sat like a guest next to the bed, included in the conversation by Auntie to confirm statements, "Didn't, she, Evelyn?" or supply information, "Wasn't she from out at——?" or linked with Auntie, "Evelyn and I were favored by. . .," in a way that made my mother smile politely. At other times Evelyn performed intimate services, as when Auntie said tactfully to her guests, "You'll have to excuse us for a few minutes."

That might be the cue for some guests to leave, but my grandmother, who had grown up partly in that house, led the way downstairs into a high-ceilinged living room, where we could look at faded sepia stereopticon pictures of places nobody in the family had been: Paris, Brussels, Niagara Falls. Or we might pull up the green shades to show the cars on a sun-bleached downtown street that had been laid out wide so the enormous freight wagons of the nineteenth century could turn around. After the woman came to invite us back upstairs, there might be a roll of toilet paper on the nightstand and, visible through the door into the bathroom, a washed bedpan propped up against the old claw-footed tub.

The woman's physical care for Auntie made her seem almost like a daughter, except that if she had been, my grandmother, for whom family were the valued of the world, would have behaved quite differently towards her.

Afterwards I asked my mother, "Is she Auntie's nurse?"

"She's not a nurse." My mother meant an R. N.

"A companion?" I tried, from my precocious reading of nineteenth-century novels.

"Oh, no. You would not call her that."

When I said, "Why not?" she didn't answer. "So what *is* she?"

"She takes care of Auntie," my mother said with finality, as if no name could be assigned to such a person.

From visits elsewhere over the years, I inferred a category of able-bodied white women who "lived in" and took care of invalid old people who could, sometimes barely, afford it. Stories attached to these women. "That man!" my grandmother said to my mother after we had left through a screened porch stacked nearly solid with yellowed newspapers, on a visit to a female step-relation of my grandmother's who was also attended by one of these women. My grandmother told a long tale about the loss of a family farm—whose, I didn't understand at first. Stories of wrong clung to these women, someone else's or their own. In another town where the caretaker of a speechless patient had been voluble, my mother clopped down the wooden front steps hissing to my sister and me, "Widow, she claims! Grass widow, more likely," and would not explain the term, but I was old enough to look it up in the dictionary.

4

How to explain those women's hold on my memory but the ambitious, emigrant life of my father from small town to city and state to state? My parents had left those towns believing they should, but never doubting that the rich and constricting life they had known there was the only right one. So it continued in them, even as it changed in those places themselves, and my parents, unable to respect the new places they went, never quite learned to live anywhere in the changing present. That cast me out from the family early into the larger world, and my business with those towns is in some wise the unfinished business of my parents.

Years later, when I was in college in the third distant city, I understood from reading Virginia Woolf that those remembered upper servants of the old were daughters of the middle class who, from fault or accident, had lost home and livelihood and lacked any skills beyond home nursing or housekeeping to earn their way in the world. As I knew them, they seem to have been disqualified from rearing other people's children—maybe by a puritan conflation of misfortune with sin or by the small-group fear of wrong associations—but to have been qualified—by race, this would've been—for the charge of helpless white elders, who were presumably beyond bad influences. Still later, after I graduated and, having long since transgressed with the rest of the world against my parents' only right way to live, had no home to return to but the ones I made for myself, I felt as if I was just a college degree and a few decades of change from having been one of these women.

5

Trees and the products of trees: the creak and sough of pines high over-head, the crack of cones onto a wood-shingled roof, the thud and crash of dead-falls in a high wind, and the faint, omnipresent scent that glanced off cold skin or worked its way into the pores of hot. These were among the first things Evelyn had known. Sticky sap that welled clear from trunks and branches and mysteriously blackened on hands and clothing; the rusty pine duff, springy on the paths, crushed to dirt on the floorboards of the house. When she was big enough to hold a broom, her job was to sweep it up from the pegged and bees-waxed floor. Her life was full of wood: the faint dry clatter of a loose-jointed doll her Opa carved for her; the smoothness of chairs she climbed up onto; the rough barrels her Papi coopered in the winter, cutting staves, beveling, soak-ing, bending them into the iron hoops.

Seeing the barrel staves, themselves soaking in a barrel, she asked, "What did they soak them in before there were any barrels?"

Augustus Kunkle laughed but never said. What was in that world was.

The pines were a dark streak on the prairie that might've been invented but did not have to be, a forest twelve miles by half a mile, where several home-steads lay. The scrap of a prehistoric forest that once covered the southern shoulder of the continent from the Atlantic Ocean to Central Texas, where the climate dried, the western edge died off, but a growth of trees survived—pos-sibly a metaphor in their searching out of ancient water under a sandstone dome—with tap roots as long as they were tall. The earliest immigrants to the area, descendants of antique Asians, camped in the pines for coolness and concealment and the shallow river that reflected a bright pathway through the woods. Later, European immigrants built houses there for nearness to pasture and farmland. One of them had been Evelyn's great-grandfather, a free-thinking socialist cabinetmaker who read Latin and Greek and fled Germany with a few books after the political suppressions of 1830. In the Texas pines his descendants became Lutherans and capitalists like their neighbors.

Once when Evelyn's father was adding a room to the house with fresh, aromatic pine lumber hauled on a mule-drawn wagon from a saw-mill, miles east, he ripped a plank off the outside of the house and showed her the wall of a pine log cabin underneath. "They never tore them down, just built around them." This was not quite true, though she did not say so: she had seen one used as it was, for a stable.

6

The woodworking of sardonic August Kunkle enabled him to keep his competent acreage debt free. A contrarian above all, he preferred woodworking but, if he had been able to devote himself to it, he might've preferred farming. A life that accommodated his preferences would've disappointed him. He was restless and worked even more than the ordinary farmer at something all the time. His wife Marina had a baby every two or three years. Evelyn was the fifth child but the first girl; she would be the middle child of nine and grew up big-eyed and self-valuing in her role as *Mamichen*.

When she was seven—this became a family story—and gathering eggs in the chill morning while minding four-year-old Liesel, the turkey Big Thomas sailed down from a low branch, fanned a white-scalloped tail, and, whistling and hissing and puffing out iridescent feathers, strutted towards them, "Get out of here," Evelyn cried and, when he ignored her, ran for the snake-killing hoe propped by the gate.

He stretched out his wattled neck and half-flew at Liesel, who sat suddenly on the ground and screamed in the cloud of dust and feathers and sharp, phosphorous dung. This was Evelyn's moment in the story, how he strode up to Liesel—they saw the round expressionless eyes, the nubby blue face, the peaked cruel beak—but Evelyn stuck the hoe between him and Liesel, and he turned majestically away, wings sweeping the dust.

What a brave *Mamichen*, the others said, what a good girl.

Since being good seemed to Evelyn no part of why she had done as she had, she began to ponder what made her good and what if she was not? Sometimes, passing the door of the eating room, she glanced in where, in a shadowy corner amid pine walls rubbed smooth and stained and gleaming, sat a strange, disused family antique. Also of pine, this was a kind of stocks built by her grandfather for disciplining his sons because he did not believe in whipping them. Turned rungs bent into the graceful curves of a chair, finely finished, with a small floorless, doorless cabinet mounted on the high back to enclose the head of the occupant, so he could look only straight in front of him—or inward on his faults. A shaped slat latched across his shoulders to keep him from leaning forward; another one with two half-holes in it latched down over the ends of the arm rests. A child sentenced to a period in the chair was not to be spoken to or fed. At Evelyn's house the chair seemed merely to belong in the eating room, but at Opa's house, Papi said, it had sat in the eating room so that the offender, ignored and hungry, could consider the privilege of shared food, for which all labored.

Father, your very father, August said in his sarcastic way, *was twice sentenced to a Sunday afternoon in that chair.*

"What had you done, Papi?"

"I spoke disrespectfully to my father."

Surely that was rude of him, Evelyn thought, but why was it wrong? "Honor thy father" was in the Bible, but so were a lot of rules nobody followed anymore.

She could read by the time she started to school. She had a mild, thoughtful temperament and pale skin that tanned only a little in the Texas summer, then resisted the sun. Her gravity and the bony angularity of her face suggested an early Renaissance churchman as rendered in a portrait, though her dark braids belonged to an idea of the farm girl. In the kitchen with her mother, she shucked and shelled and peeled and hulled as she minded the little ones and wondered why everything, to be useful, had to be separated from something else.

At school, she learned spelling, arithmetic, history as dates (1776, 1812, 1836, 1861), geography as facts ("the Nile, the longest river in the world," "the Alps, the highest mountains in the world"), and literature as elevating thoughts ("Breathes there the man with soul so dead . . .?"), herself teaching Liesel to read while studying at the kitchen table, as her next older brother Al had taught her.

7

On the morning she had made the potato salad for the picnic, she was minding Liesel, who was six then, and Greta, who was three, because Mami was nursing Bea, who was the baby. They had been sent out into the yard to cut branches of bright pink azalea to take to the cemetery, and when they were through, they were to go inside, wash, and dress in the spring dresses Mami had sewed them for Homecoming.

Homecoming in 1919 in Iron Rock was a day of somber ceremony unconnected to schools or football games. A day celebrated instead of the impossible Decoration Day—that Southern memorial for the Civil War dead—or the even more impossible federal Memorial Day, because there had been men in Central Texas not sixty years before who had refused to swear the oath of allegiance to the Confederacy. Some had been shot or hanged by Confederate vigilantes from trees people could still point out. Some had escaped to fight for the Union. A sizeable party had fought their pursuers on their way to Mexico, and some, forced to surrender, had been massacred by militia. Many other men of Central Texas, seeing no difficulty or no practical choice over a Confederacy dedicated to slaveholding, had fought for it. How to memorialize communally such various dead? In the future elsewhere of easy destruction, their descendants might've blown up public places in the neighborhoods of the old enemy. At Homecoming each family joined its neighbors to clean up the cemetery, decorate such graves as they chose to, and share a quiet picnic, which seemed to be mainly about the common experience of having had ancestors they did not choose and being subject to die.

The telephone they called the shouting telephone rang from the wall in the hallway, and the children in the yard heard Papi answer it and stopped piling up branches of azalea. They picked at the insect-like antennae of the flowers, and waited: the telephone often meant bad news.

When Papi came out onto the porch, he announced, "We will not go to the cemetery today. Uncle Jakob found a dead woman under the brush arbor in the cemetery."

What difference did that make? Evelyn would remember thinking, the cemetery was all dead people, and about the potato salad she had labored over. The brush arbor, which provided shade for burial services, was where the tables for the picnic were set up.

Later, Papi and Gus and Fred and Kurt did go to the cemetery, with the men and older boys of other households for a few hours' work. But women and children did not go, and most children were kept from knowing more, that day. They found out in time, as older boys told the news, confidentially or cruelly, *You know what they found?* and other children repeated it. *They say.*

Jakob Schlegel had volunteered that year to haul the sawhorses and boards for the picnic tables out to the brush arbor and set them up. Early in the morning he and two teenage sons, one of them to become a local historian, had loaded the heavy boards and sawhorses onto a mule wagon and driven out to the cemetery.

From the reddish clay of the cemetery road that looped around on treeless bottom land the man and the two boys could see something on the ground under the brush arbor. *It looked like a bundle of clothes,* Ernest Schlegel would write, *roped there at the corner to one of the uprights of the frame.*

Father was grim. "Whoa," he said, "whoa. Stay in the wagon."

The brush arbor lay, as old-timers will remember, at some distance from the road.

Father got down and went in under the brush arbor and stood over the bundle, waving flies from his face, and when we stood up in the wagon, we saw it was a person. He reached out with the butt of his driving whip and lifted long hair, and we saw it was a woman, and he took off his hat and held it over his heart, as if at graveside at funerals, and we did the same with ours. The ground around the body was dark.

"A woman has been murdered," he said when he came back, and that there could be no picnic there that day. He drove to town, straight to the undertaker's and we sat there in the wagon while he went in.

We did not know any more until he drove to the pastor's and the pastor came with us to the church, and we got down and scythed the back yard, where the grass was long and green with the spring. Then we unloaded the tables and set them up there. Other men stopped by to help, and we heard them talking: the woman had been whipped to death; she had been "in a family way," as they said in those days; Father had seen the baby in her belly, which was cut open by the whip. He had not—in that moment when he lifted her hair from her face—recognized her.

The body was laid out at the undertaker's, the indentation of a wedding ring said to have marked her finger, and all day people were asked to go and look, in hopes of identifying her. But if anybody knew who she was, they did not say, though she or the man who had killed her—nobody doubted it was a man—must've had some connection around Iron Rock. Or why take her to the cemetery on the night before Homecoming to kill her?

A little older, Evelyn would ponder that question with other girls, what the man thought the woman had done and whether she had done it or, most horribly of all, hadn't. But for a long while what Evelyn would remember most sharply about Homecoming 1919 would be her disappointment of the morning and her discovery that evening, at the picnic held behind the church. In the spring chill that sundown floated onto them like a cold damp cloth, she and her sisters and the other girls had been playing the sing-song, "Go in and out the windows," twirling between the arcs of joined hands moving through the altered air, "As we have done this day."

Collapsed warm into a wooden folding chair, Evelyn heard a woman muse to Mami, "—and nobody with the slightest idea who."

"I've seen that deep-browed look," Mami said, "with the eyes close to-gether." It was, the two women agreed, a look some people had.

"Shh," Mami said.

So that Evelyn, who had never slept in a bed alone or been long out of sight or sound of familiar others, sprawled back amid the whine of early mosquitoes and sought the night sky for the seven sisters, trying to imagine dying where she knew nobody and nobody knew her.

8

Three families, Kunkles, Gants, and McCoys, lived along Kunkle Road, which ran along the edge of the pines and dried after wet spells into head-jarring, axle-cracking ruts and would be graded when it got too bad—in the road-labor every household owed the county—by whichever family borrowed the blade. This road was named for its first destination, but the wear of feet and hooves and wagon wheels had extended it to Gants' and later McCoys', *after the McCoys stopped making whiskey and came down out of the hills. So* that Evelyn Kunkle had always known Les Gant, the oldest of the Gant brothers—they had no sisters to take care of them, poor things. Their family land bordered the Kunkles' on one side, and Les, her brother Kurt's fishing friend, was four years older than she was. He was at their house sometimes, when members of the family sat outside in the evening on rough seats hewn from big logs, in a fenced and grassless yard covered with brown pine needles, and the boys got up with knives to cut hard amber chews from the wellings of trees.

The oldest of five sons of the biggest landowner, Les Gant was a leader but also cautious, serious, and such a good student that he had hopes of going off to the agricultural college. His father, a big broad man who insisted on being called Lester, boasted of these hopes; he ran his sons like a work gang but he never kept them out of school for it. Maybe because Les seemed destined to go away, at the time in Evelyn's life when country girls first begin to look around them and wonder who they might marry she was kept from thinking of Les Gant.

9

Old German farmer: *You can't eat it*. Old German farmer with a mortgage: *Fifty acres, fifty bales, a hundred dollars a bale*.

In the rainy period they had waited for, that spring Les went out every dawn to the moist field, hunkered down with fingertips on a row of the reddish soil, and looked closely. He was the first to see the sprouts break the soil; they looked like his future. He did chores, pried off muddy boots on the back step and, in the kitchen where his mother stood at the wood range, ate a bowl of cornmeal mush with new milk, two potato pancakes, and three fried eggs, before driving his four brothers off to school—what were they arguing about?— in the big Studebaker, feeling half gone from the place already.

Les was the first to see the lobed leaves of the cotton seedlings open, and the only one who crouched in the morning-damp field to see stem nodes budded out before the nubs of stalks began to grow. As the plants grew into dark-green bushes, he waded along an outer row regularly, measuring them against his long denim shins. He was the first to see signs of flower buds: "It's squaring," he announced triumphantly.

On the pearly morning when the squares began to open into big white blowsy flowers, Marvin, who had come with him on a bet, chanted the old riddle: "First day white, second day red"— *pink* would not've rhymed—"third day of my life, I'm—."

"—a cotton boll," Les interposed.

"Ain't money pretty?"

"Isn't." Les seized him in a hammerlock. "Say it right."

They were seventeen and fifteen, Les the do-right, Marvin the scapegrace, and Marvin could not imagine life without his older brother, though he had to admit the son-of-a gun ought to go to college. He wasn't the most charming fellow—that would be Marvin—but Les could sure pay attention to things.

Les was the first to discover holes in the petals, too, and weevils, feeding on the pollen. *Always a few.* With their tiny goggle eyes and nozzle snouts they looked like gas masks from the European war. Les worked his way down a row, picking them off, popping them with his thumb nail; there weren't many.

Well, the first time I did see him, Marvin sang unmusically, *He was walking on the square.*

"Always a few," their father said.

Les would've had his brothers picking every weevil if his father had let him. No, Lester said, they'd knock as many flowers off as they saved and, "Corn before cotton"—in the timeless priority of food for humans and animals—they had to cultivate the corn before the Johnson grass got hold.

It was like the time a first-calf heifer was having a hard time calving and Les's father wouldn't call the vet. *That calf's going to die.*

You teaching me the cow-calf business?

In the birdsong dawns amid rows of thigh-high bushes, Les found cotton bolls with the wart-like blemishes of eggs; bolls with their tangle of developing filaments spotted brown with decay and in each spot, a wormlike larva. *Too many.* Grudging every boll, he picked the yellowing bolls off two adjoining rows, but he couldn't do the field by himself.

In June there were boll weevils on almost every plant, and Marvin sang bitterly, *Well the second time I seen him, he'd brought his family there.*

Then they were all carrying feed sacks down the rows, picking weevils, picking blistered and holey and yellowed bolls, tying the sacks up tight with binder's twine, and carrying them to the river. "Wonder if fish'd bite on the big 'uns," Marvin said.

"Open that sack, and I'll break your arm." They drowned the sacks in the river.

At the beginning of July, it was there to do all over again, only, on the hottest afternoon of the year so far, they built a fire of litter at the edge of the field. Watching the air above it shrivel, they threw their bags in. "Did you see that?" Marvin said.

"That black smoke?"

"That was no smoke, *bruder.* That was the weevils flying out of one sack, back to the rows."

"*Bruder,* yourself. That was my sack and it had engine oil on it."

Just a-looking for a home, Marvin sang, *just a-looking for a home.*

They made a few bales but not enough to send Les to college. He put a brave face on it—"I can learn it on my own"—and his father gave him a section of pasture to manage and a bred heifer, as he would give each of his sons when he graduated from high school. *Reckons Marvin won't graduate, otherwise.*

Secretly Les aspired to equaling, in a different way, his father's improvement of their land. Lester Gant, who had inherited his several thousand exhausted acres young and alone, had brought them back from ruin by working days building rock houses to buy guano and going home at night to clear brush by lantern light. Such heroism was not to be thought of, but Les subscribed to two farm magazines, was often seen talking with the County Agent, and began trying to talk his father out of cotton, into stock farming entirely. It was, Les dared to say, the future.

As to the rest of his personal future, he took for granted marriage and a large family of sons—he meant to have daughters, too, whom he imagined as slim, hard-working, definite young versions of his mother—but he did not flirt with girls as Marvin did. Girls flirted with Les, and he marveled at that different, girl way they had of looking at you, and how their hair sat up off their faces. When they stood next to him, the soft billows and hollows of their bodies became all he could think of, and he did not know what to say to them, though he never had that problem with boys or men. Marvin in a blowhard mood might've called himself "a man's man"; Les rejected the phrase as pretentious. Fortunately, the girls who flirted with him took care of the conversation, and, for his part, he invited some of them to social events, never any one often enough that anybody might expect anything.

10

Evelyn, with her pale skin and big eyes grew into—not prettiness, with the length of her nose and the thinness of her face—but a look of distinction and refinement: the straight way she held herself, the thin supple hands that reminded you of her mother's people, the Schlegels, among whom were musicians locally well-known. They had played in the municipal and fraternal bands from before the radio; they played in churches, directed choirs, taught music. Evelyn was not a musician, but she loved being a Schlegel-Kunkle, loved the purity and clarity of certain musical tones, which were like the tastes of ice and fresh mint at Aunt Gainer's or the sharp brilliant greens and blues of Aunt Charlotte's embroidery thread. All of these things, like the smells of clean sheets, clean clothes, and clean babies, belonged to an identity she held secret, right there in public.

The spring Evelyn Kunkle was seventeen, when with still only eleven grades in public school she was about to graduate valedictorian of her class, Les Gant, slim, eagle-faced, silent, and twenty-one, began to court her. He made his intentions clear enough, saying abruptly early on that his father had married when he was twenty-two. Evelyn was not talkative either, but they knew each other's families and friends and places and regular work so well that the details of getting together and doing something provided all the subjects for talk that seemed necessary. She had never had an admirer before and the little ripple through her chest she felt at his attention seemed right, the revelation of a next necessary in life. They were alike in certain respects, hard-working, devoted to family, accustomed to being responsible for people. They fit comfortably enough going to barbecues on hot green afternoons, drifting down the long twilights of church suppers together, presenting themselves together in the candle-light and lamp glow of rare winter parties, submitting in a new spring to the fraught awkwardness of flowered weddings.

On a late-summer Sunday afternoon, they went swimming in woolen bathing suits at fish camp, that shared place of family memory, where Les

dived off the small pier and his big tawny cow dog dived in after him. Drop-
lets flying in sparkles off the ends of Les's fingers, they swam down the watery
avenue of sun through the pines. Not to be bested by a dog, Evelyn followed,
easing in off the end of the pier, splashing effortfully through the water; she
had not swum since she was a child, although Kurt and Al had taught her at
that very place. They had all learned to swim at fish camp, and to fish, too:
Kunkles and Gants, also McCoys—on whose land it happened to lie—and
because fish camp had been Les's considered choice that day and will become
a major setting in this story, I pause here over its qualities.

Chief among them was its communality, in a region otherwise familial.
Before fish camp had been a particular place, it had been a shared time. In
late summer, when the cotton on family farms had grown too thick to hoe for
weeds, people would get up a fishing trip with the neighbors. They levered
big black wash pots up onto a wagon bed, lined others with quilts and mat-
tresses, piled on bags of cornmeal, buckets of home-made lard, croker sacks
jumbled full of coffee pots and eating utensils; they drove along a river road to
a cut-through such as the one off Kunkle Road that in time became Fish Camp
Road. A clearing along the riverbank offered a low place to climb down, grav-
elly shallows above a sudden drop-off, a deep hole. Women set themselves and
the children up to fish for bait perch off cane poles; men stripped pine saplings
and drilled the stobs into the bank to fish for the opelousa cat called *yellow*.
Fires were built, lard melted in a wash pot, the catch was filleted out from the
strange branching bones, and people who lived on cornbread and salt meat
and home-grown vegetables gorged themselves on fried fish, fresh as it came.
At night, the older boys tracked the pulsing deep resonance of bullfrogs by
lantern light, while children went to sleep in wagon beds, looking up and falling into the deep starry sky. Adults sat up late talking, drawing on pipes that
illuminated both men's and women's faces in the dense darkness.

Motor vehicles ended fish camp as a time. When people could pile the family into the car and go see the Gulf or the mountains, fish camp became a place.
A fixed place to swim, string a trot line or a throw line, get off for a few hours'
fishing by yourself; a shared, traditional place to run into the neighbors and
talk about improvements, such as the small pier Les had dived from or the
refuge of the Kunkle-Gant-McCoy screen-wire shack from the mosquitoes. An
emblem of the shared past and life, for which I imagine Les as having chosen it

on this occasion, knowing that without having had to think it at all.

Any more than, when he turned around to swim back up the other side of the river, he had to think about passing the dog and Evelyn, so as to lead them in tandem past the secret, snaky-looking places made by pine branches drooping out over the water, or than Evelyn had to think about rearranging herself to follow him directly, or than the dog had to think about ceasing to separate them and taking his place behind her.

Opposite the climb-out, they swam across, put their feet down on the submerged limestone shelf, and stood, Evelyn neck-deep in the tea-colored water, white shoulders shining through. A vehicle growled its way along Kunkle Road, and though fish-camp was only a half mile from it and anybody could've come, they felt alone and Les kissed her—was this the way you did it?—their lips still cool from the water. He did not say anything about love, nobody in either of their families did, as if it might be too sacred to mention, or the expression inadequate to the fact, or the fact irrelevant to the daily performance, but Les was stirred up and supposed what he felt was love for her. As he had planned on doing, he asked her to marry him.

A drop of water slid down the side of her face; she brushed it away. Of course she said yes: three of her four older brothers were married and gone; the fifth, Al, talked about staying at home to take care of the old folks and the young ones; and there was no boy Evelyn liked better than Les Gant.

11

"A rock house," declared Lester, as the two fathers sat on the front porch of the one he had built for his own bride, rusty brown and tan and palomino river rock. "Cool in summer."

And cold in winter, August Kunkle thought but said only, "A generous gift." *Auf Deutsch, das Gift meint* poison, he recalled, although this was more about his outlook than about the occasion. "Quarry or river?"

"I'm thinking, quarry." The difference was about the shapes of rocks, which was about how you built with them.

"Frame walls inside," August offered. "Save you a form."

"Gus, you just got to get that wood in there, don't you?"

"I build the in," he said, and refrained from adding, *Whereas you only build a stone wall around it.*

The two men had been acquainted all their lives. August Kunkle thought Lester Gant, who owned twice as much land as he did, was land-proud and wrong-headedly ambitious, and Lester Gant thought August Kunkle was a superior son-of-a-bitch. But Kunkles and Gants had been good neighbors for nearly ninety years and in every generation taught their sons to be, above almost everything else, good neighbors. They shared a boundary, kept up their fences, never disputed a right-of-way or the acts of an animal; so important were these matters to country prosperity that good neighborliness was nearly sacred. Their wives were friends to the extent that country wives had time to be, various of their children were friends, and, in some combination, a marriage in the two families had seemed likely since the generation represented by August and Lester had begun to produce children. All the same, on social occasions the two men greeted each other with wary remarks about crops or cattle or the electric companies' refusal to run lines to rural customers, before turning away to different conversations. The longest talk they'd had in years before this one had been about the maintenance of the dock at fish camp, for which they shared responsibility with Ian McCoy, who could no longer be relied on for anything but trouble. A neighbor like that—Gant's burden, not Kunkle's—made a man appreciate a good one.

"I reckon to build the house in that old clearing down there." Lester pointed towards the end of the driveway.

Where the old Gant house stood, August did not say, lest he seem to sneer at the family history. That ambitious house, even its rock foundation broken up and excavated for other uses now, had been built by the settler Gants, whom the settler Kunkles had dismissed as get-rich-quick people, along with the rest of the Southerners who arrived driving that affront to free white labor, a gang of enslaved blacks. For a few years, the captives had stripped prairie and cultivated big acreages of cotton, earning for their masters enormous sums, already owed, of course, some on those very captives. Then it all crashed, as men of moral discernment had known it must do, and the creditors with it; and the land, afterwards sharecropped by the hard-pressed for the otherwise shiftless, had been allowed to go slowly to brush. If anybody had been able to buy land in those times when, thanks to that old foolishness, the only credit was the crop-lien, some Gant would have sold off the property in pieces. At the moral nadir of the family, a young Gant, fallen to barroom gambler, had been hanged for robbery of his neighbors by local vigilantes—Kunkles among them—though whether justly no one could now say.

And then, out of all that arrogance and wastrel idleness, had sprung up Lester Gant, who, freed early of the older generation and perhaps learning from observing his neighbors, had not been too fine a gentleman to work with his hands. He had labored early and late to reclaim his ruined acres. He had married a good German girl and fathered five sons, all of whom had lived. He was known for telling his children early the story of the Gant black sheep: *What people think of you, and your family, matters.* People, in fact, stood somewhat in awe of Lester Gant, for his luck, resolve, and physical strength. August Kunkle's disdain for him was, at the distance they kept, philosophical.

They maintained this distance through the joint building of Les's house. On Sunday mornings during the fall, the labor-rich Gants dug and poured the foundation—the Gants having also in common with the Kunkles only occasional churchgoing. Art and Chet and Parker Gant, wearing red kerchiefs like bandits, poured sand and cement into a wooden box, and, as the dust plumed up to settle on the oil drums full of water they had hauled, Les wielded the broken hoe.

"Mix it up good, boys," Lester said, "before you add the water."

When the foundation was cured August Kunkle brought Al to help him raise the rooftree but mostly climbed and shuffled around by himself, framing and raising the pine walls, which later he would finish out. Seeing him squinting and measuring and consulting the intricate drawings he made for all sorts of projects, Les had stopped to ask whether he needed any help, but all he got for it was the old man's ironic smile. Which Les did not deserve, because he did all the plumbing on the Gant place and would plumb the new house, but his father-in-law to be was, as Kurt Kunkle had always said, an odd duck.

By early winter the Gants had laid the rock corners around old August Kunkle's walls, with Lester going on telling them how to do it even after they knew. One Sunday morning he declared the obvious, "Now we got to go through the pile and find the rest of the big 'uns, to go along the bottom."

Chet rolled his eyes, as Chet would do, and Les granted him the commiserating look, because straw bossing for Lester was the extra job laid on

Les. "Well, let's get after it," Les said. *Get After It,* Parker claimed, was Les's middle name.

But if it was a question of moving rock, then where was Marvin?—who was big and broad like Lester and could heave any weight. "Still in bed," Les said, "last I saw him." Marvin drove the family truck to dances for miles around and came in at all hours. "Look to me like he'd been in a fight." The old man snorted a laugh, though he damn sure wouldn't have if it was Les disabled himself for a morning's work.

The rest of them had nearly separated the pile into two piles before Marvin showed up, with both eyes blackened and a story. "Thought I could whip that feller, but I sure was wrong." Les managed to lay two big rocks and mortar them in while Marvin was still telling the story.

"You ought to quit running around and marry that girl," Les told him, but Marvin said she'd wait.

"Wet the rocks," Lester said, "it sticks better," and the younger brothers exchanged their glance. One of their jokes was that Lester was so full of authority the five of them were hardly enough for him to exercise it on.

Les said he reckoned they were doing that.

12

"*Schaetzchen,* you should be asleep," Evelyn whispered when eleven-year-old Greta in white-smocked nightgown crept into the parlor: Mami was asleep in a small adjoining room, formerly the sewing room. The old black treadle sewing machine with its painted gold flourishes had been moved into the parlor, and Evelyn sat in front of it, but it was noisy to pedal and, sitting up late to work on her wedding dress, she was only basting organdy ruffles.

"I'll miss you," Greta complained. She climbed onto the chintz cushion in Mami's rocking chair and began to rock. "When you move to Les's house."

"It's *our* house, darling."

Greta rocked until the chair traveled over the floor. "Don't, you'll wake Mami." Mami, who now slept alone, had been unwell since Sammy was born. "I won't be far at all. You can come over any time."

Greta sighed and sucked on the end of a braid. "Do you sit down here dreaming about having Les Gant's babies?"

"Oh, Greta. What an idea." Evelyn had tended too many babies to need to dream about them. She stuck pins into a faded orange pin cushion shaped like a pumpkin. "But I remember when *you* were born, I was seven, being driven to Aunt Charlotte's. I had to look after Liesel and we were so excited."

Greta let go of her braid and said out loud, "I remember when Bea was born." Evelyn put a finger to her lips. "We went to Aunt Charlotte's and it sleeted." Evelyn remembered: Gus was away in the army, and Fred was allowed to stay at home to do chores.

"I'm glad we had Sammy."

Evelyn, who was too, smiled and whispered, "Go back to bed, I'm coming right up."

But she sat on for a few minutes downstairs, finishing her seam and wondering whether she ought to be dreaming about having babies: was that what engaged girls did? For a strange moment she might not even have wanted to marry. But of course, she did. Who chose to be an old maid?

Upstairs in the girls' room she put on her nightgown and, as she climbed carefully into bed with Bea, who was already folded up sound asleep, Evelyn tried to imagine getting into bed with hard-bodied Les Gant. She lay on clean white sheets that smelled faintly of pine and sunlight and tried to imagine what married people did in bed. All her life, she had seen the nannies going down on their elbows to the billies, the bull jumping the cows, with that big thing flopping blind. But she had thought of that as only nature, until once, beginning to round the corner of the chicken coop, she had glimpsed Al back there with it in his hand—so much bigger than baby Sammy's, her first thought had been, what was that?—but she had been driven back by his furtive hunch and the intensity of his absorption. She had stood listening to the hard fast scour of fabric against fabric, and at his long, groaning sigh, she had seemed to understand everything: how much male creatures craved to exercise that part of themselves, and why keeping a man from getting even close to it with a woman until they were married was up to the woman, *Or the babies would be all in the wrong places.*

Of the female genitalia she knew only in the expression, *down there,* as in: *Be sure to wash down there,* which she always had, and, *Don't ever fool with anything down there,* which she never had. *Don't ever let a boy touch you down there*, had astonished her, that a boy would want to, until she understood. *After you're married you have to let your husband do what he wants to down there.*

13

So here emerge the newly married Mr. and Mrs. Les Gant in—early June, say—1927, from the Lutheran church, Les in the shiny new boots and crisp tie that made up his wedding finery, Evelyn in the dress of closely-sewn organdy ruffles and the wreath of pistillate flowers she had chosen instead of a veil, which seemed to her ancient, Oriental, uncivilized. How young she looks! How upright and self-contained he! Squinting in the same moment of sun, how little they know each other's private selves, or will in the ten years of their marriage, a confident, reasonable, and widely approved union designed for devastation. If my fiction is cruel in creating such a union it is, at least in this way, undistinguished from life.

For Evelyn there were the more or less expected wedding-night surprises, beginning when she and Les got into bed between the soft old linen sheets that had belonged to Oma Schlegel. Les put his hand *down there* and felt around as if he knew little more about it than Evelyn did, and after he got on top of her, he had to probe for the place again with an uncertain finger. When he stuck that part of himself in, it was like being split open all the way up, not just at the hymen, as she had thought. But it was over so quickly that, lying there afterwards in the new room listening to an irregular ticking from some source she could not identify, Evelyn felt the irony of the fuss people made about it: all of nature and society organized around the slight moments of that act.

For Les, there were no wedding night surprises, not that he had expected any from Evelyn. He had known to be patient with his bride's response to the marital act—*but watch out after that first baby*, an old man with ears so finely haired they looked feathery had confided slyly at the reception in the fellowship hall. Les had been more worried about the sounds of vehicles on the Gant driveway, voices approaching through the woods that would represent a mutiny led by Marvin. Partly because of who Les was, a shivaree—that old-fashioned interruption of the wedding night with shooting and shouting and clattering of spoons on pans—had been planned for him, but that morning

Marvin had come down to tell Les that Lester had put a stop to it.

Les, who had moved himself into the new house and was already dressed to go to church, was out in the flourishing green of a summer garden he had cultivated for his bride, poking along looking for caterpillars amid the rough leaves and curling tendrils of bean plants he could get at without dirtying his boots.

"What he said"—Marvin was glum—"'Let the boy get on with his business.' But

hell. . .."

It was a social mistake on Lester's part, they both knew it. Les would get to that other business soon enough, but meanwhile what about the boys?

This name they called themselves almost said it: their yet-to-be elevation to adult privileges, their loss of Les as one of them on the occasion of his marriage. Ambivalence about it deserved to be acknowledged. The shivaree, as practiced by the Gant, Kunkle, and McCoy brothers and some of their single cousins and other neighbors, obliged the groom to come out of his house on his wedding night and treat to drinks for as long as they chose to stay. Marvin, the natural organizer of such events, had purchased the illegal whiskey for Les to do so.

"Think you ought to say something to him?" Marvin suggested. Nobody else could do that much, and the only matter Les had succeeded in getting his father to even listen to him about—getting out of cotton—had taken several years with still-limited effect.

On the day of Les's wedding, with the gift of the rock house and the designation of another section of land for his exclusive cultivation, Les would receive from Lester as much independence as he probably ever would as long as they both lived on the place. He had been treated with magnanimity, and Lester might or might not repeat it with the younger boys.

As usual, Marvin had withheld the worst for last: "Reckon the word's already out. Al called up to ask" if the old man had, in fact, forbidden it.

Les threw up his hands. "And you want me to ask him to back down in public? Not going to happen. No way, no how."

"Not even ask?"

Least of all to Marvin could Les say, *Not with everything he's given me.* "Would you want to fight him on your wedding day?"

The silent mouth of Marvin's disgust said Les had failed him, and, after he went away, Les knew he had failed all the boys in some final responsibility. Then when Marvin, at the altar as best man, handed him the ring, his closed, rebellious face made Les wonder whether he had yielded at all, risky fellow that he was. So that after the consummation of his marriage, Les drowsed off in renewed dread of the forbidden shivaree.

It never came. The surprises following his marriage took months to develop, the chief being how little marriage changed a person's membership in a family. A woman changed her name, changed where she lived. As for the rest, Les had known the Kunkles were different from the Gants—it had seemed to be why his father and old August didn't like each other any better than they did—but Les had somehow imagined the marriage would take care of that difference insofar as it might affect the two of them. For six months after the wedding, he thought it had: he and Evelyn ate Sunday dinner at the Gants' and his brothers joked about finally having a sister. True, she was a little stiff with them, but they were a lot to take, ganged up like that. True, she slipped off through the woods "to see Mami and the *kleinen*," more often than Les would've liked. But the two of them ate the Gants' Thanksgiving turkey with them and, when the weather got cold enough, killed hogs with the Gants, Evelyn making *wurst* to his mother's recipe and brining bacon and hams with the rest of them as if she had always done it. She even remarked to him afterwards that it was "just a different old man fussy about how he smoked the meat."

So that, to go to the Kunkles' on Christmas Eve seemed only fair. But, as preparations for the widely known Schlegel-Kunkle Christmas pageant required Les and Evelyn's repeated presence, along with that of a number of other family members, Les was mildly repelled by what the old people called their *Weihnachtsspiel*, He had never been to it before, let alone seen the effort that went into it. "They do this every year?" he said to Evelyn, and she laughed. "Every year." Evelyn had been honored with the part of Mary, so Les must play "St. Joseph the Protector," as Aunt Gainer instructed him in rehearsals. Kurt, who was one of the Three Kings, lived too far away for rehearsals.

On Christmas Eve in the Kunkles' frigid barn, Les stood with a rough woolen robe tied over his clothes and a cloth tied around his head feeling about like as much of a burro as the one tethered to the upright, while Evelyn sat in a blue robe looking at her youngest nephew asleep on the hay in an old wood feeding trough. Around them, members of her family who had *wanted* parts this year had arranged themselves on Xs chalked on the barn floor. There was Old August in a hooded brown robe out front and center, wielding a turkey quill like a pen as a gospel writer for an audience of relatives in borrowed wooden folding chairs who had either not wanted or somehow gotten out of having to participate this year.

And there knelt the married brothers August, Frederick, and Kurt, in fine white turbans, wearing robes with hanging embroidered parts like church vestments. Mami, off to the side in a tinsel halo and long white quilted, silver-embroidered wings, sang *glorias* in a truly unearthly soprano, echoed by the sisters Liesel, Greta, and Beatrice, and the sisters-in-law and nieces and female cousins down the smallest children, all in tinsel halos and puffy white wings, which Les was glad to learn had not all been made this year. Somebody from an older generation had carved the time-darkened crooks carried by robed shepherds, Al among them, and a cousin who was married to a Heimsoth cousin of Les's, and Sammy, though he was only five, who had refused to be an angel. All directed by Aunt Gainer, who was a Schlegel, who gave piano lessons and had worked out a new harmony for *"Stille Nacht"* that Les had never been able to learn; he could not keep his voice from following the familiar melody.

The Germans in his mother's family were nothing like this; all the effort—and for what? It was like old August's drawings and plans for pieces of furniture he would never build, which, for sure, Evelyn laughed about. The thought that she was not too serious about it all comforted Les. Still, there had been no question that he and she, as the newlyweds, must participate in the *Weihnachtsspiel,* and the singing of his new brothers-in-law, each a solo verse of "We Three Kings," recalled to Les the Kunkle family habit of reading out loud in turn to each other, which he had not seen until he and Evelyn were courting.

He had gone over one night to take her sweater back to her and had heard from the porch a girl's voice going on in a schoolroom sort of way, and when he went in they were all sitting there and Liesel was holding the open book as if waiting to go on. Les felt unwelcome and didn't stay. Afterwards Evelyn explained that they often read like that, "passing around the book," which had been *The Last Days of Pompeii,* which sounded like history but was a novel. In the evenings, if she had no mending, she still read books like that. Les read too, of course, but only for things he might find useful to know.

He remembered to look out at the audience as he was supposed to do from time to time, and his eyes focused beyond the row of lamps on an ancient, upright, great-uncle he had been introduced to earlier, Uncle Cappy, he was called. A townsman and poor, though apparently not at all a lazy or loose-living person, he had spoken with such enthusiasm about having learned to play horns with funny names, the flugelhorn, the opich-something, he had seemed almost crazy. Like other old Schlegels, he had apparently frittered away whatever chances he might've had in life on playing and teaching music—not that Les had anything against those activities: teaching had been a valuable fallback for the widowed Aunt Gainer. But to choose such a life when young?

Recalling that he had married Evelyn, not her relatives, Les looked back at her, with her beatific smile, and supposed he could do this once a year if he couldn't get out of it. He wondered what she was thinking about, gazing at the baby, maybe the one of their own he had hoped every month since their wedding he would've started in her.

Then it was time to sing "Joy to the World," with the audience joining in; then time for the cast, keeping silence with the rest, to file out ahead into the crisp night air. Les shook Kurt's hand silently, and that was the way they did it: beforehand, cookies, Christmas tree, *Glühwein* heated with a poker; then the *Weihnachtsspiel* and this parting in silence with, after all the weeks of effort, nothing they had not had before.

On the dark woods path, the pines creaked and a disappearance of white might've been the throat of a gray fox veering away from Les's well-secured chicken-house. "That Uncle Cappy's quite a character."

"Isn't he?"

"He talked about music instruments I never heard of before."

"He lives music. He's eighty years old and he told me—he's played horns all his life—he's started learning to play the glockenspiel!" She had to explain that the glockenspiel was not a horn.

"Is he crazy?"

Evelyn laughed. "No more than the rest of them."

At least she didn't say *us*. Les recalled Kurt from before he had ranched distant McCaverty land, when he and Les had ranged the river on occasional Sundays; Kurt had seemed like anybody else. But girls, Les, knew, belonged more to a family.

At home in the bedroom, where banked embers still glowed faintly in the fireplace from the fire he had built for Evelyn to dress by because it was Christmas Eve, he said, "How beautiful you were, smiling there at the baby. What were you thinking?"

She pulled the dark green dress off over her head, a new winter Sunday dress she had made for what she called her trousseau, and he got a good look at her in the long straight slip and the treasured dress-up stockings she wore *inside out, for the dull side.*

"Of the first Christmas I can remember. I was an angel, and I primped at my wings until they came untied and fell halfway off."

Les put his arms awkwardly around her anyhow, though she broke out of them soon to put on her nightgown. She seemed to be always breaking out of his embraces to do something as, in bed after they coupled and he rolled off her, she slid out of bed to wash herself. Of course, women had sanitary needs men did not, and cleanliness was a valuable quality in a wife, so he could not tell her he wished she would stay, he would've liked for her to lie there entwined with him, drowse off with him. Lying there alone, he wondered whether she enjoyed their copulation; he could not ask her. He listened instead to the running of the bathroom tap he himself had plumbed for her and wondered whether she loved him as he did her.

14

They worked well together and were proud of doing so, although neither of them thought of saying that to the other. Evelyn's work was changed the most by marriage. At home she had done the chores that had long been hers or that she could do to save Mami's failing strength. Here, she was responsible for everything that Les wasn't: for lighting the lamps when they got up before daylight and—until they got the gas installed—building fires, spreading out the coals with the blackened Confederate sword he had found in the Gant barn for a poker, shoveling out ashes, and minding the ever-hungry woodbox, which they both worked at filling. Here, tending milk cows and chickens, making butter and cheese, preserving eggs in isinglass were all hers; also canning the year, peas-to-pumpkins, along with some of the Kunkles' peaches-to-pears that Papi brought over, saying, *because no Gant will ever devote land to fruit trees.* Here, minding the ice delivery was also hers, old man Hall's current adolescent son driving a mule wagon, as some people still did for heavy loads, because the only real refrigeration for families in the country was freezer lockers at the co-op in town, but in the pines they could get the big blocks of ice delivered, hefted into the icebox with tongs once a week, because there were enough households for that.

But the work that did not demand its own time was Evelyn's to plan—unless, as rarely, Les needed an extra hand to drive the hard-steering Gant tractor. She could choose her day to do laundry in the corrugated metal washhouse he had built for her, with water piped to faucets above two big washpots over a fire box. She could choose the strong morning to scrub the floors or the kitchen or—that least-favorite task—the chicken house, then settle down with a cup of coffee to refill the lamps. She could choose to do a thing at one instead of another time for her own convenience, as when the stove needed its regular blacking against rust and she put it off until after she'd done her ironing, because the heating flatirons were hard enough to keep clean as it was.

And the difference that made all the others, for the first three years, was that the house and yard belonged to her and Les—that and the absence of children. How she missed her Liesel and Greta, who did not come over as often as they might've, and her precious Bea and Sammy! How mindlessly she worried about them! Then, at the end of the twenties, the gas company, extending service to Iron Rock, wanted to dig across a Gant pasture with the pipeline, though they had not planned to serve rural customers at all. They offered the usual sort of insignificant lease-fee, but Lester demanded gas service to the pines instead, and after refusals, threats from the company, even—but they did not know who they were dealing with—he got it. Les piped his parents' house for gas first, then his own, and, the next year, Marvin's when they built it. After that, they all had gas lights, gas cook stoves, and clean new gas irons that could blow you up if you weren't careful.

15

Evelyn had gone up to "the house" as they called it—as if Les's and hers did not count—to take a peach pie she had made because she had a lot of Papi's peaches and Lester liked peach pie. She knew he did not much like her. Tessa waved from the window, and, as they did at each other's houses, Evelyn went into the kitchen without knocking. The well-oiled hinges of the screen door made no sound when she opened it, and just then in the adjoining bedroom, Lester growled, ". . .that sterile heifer August sold me." Evelyn heard it distinctly. *As if Papi had wanted her to marry a Gant.* She let the screendoor slam.

Tessa, used to cleaning up after her husband socially, bustled into the kitchen talking about a sack of shelled-out pecans she had for Evelyn and Les, and Evelyn set the pie down to exclaim over the pecans, and the moment seemed to have passed in these ritual reassertions. And afterwards, when Evelyn was gone, Tessa would go back in to Lester and shame him with the pie, and remind him she'd told him if he didn't quit calling Evelyn that, she was going to hear it sometime.

On her way again with the sack of pecan halves, Evelyn still burnt from the insult. *As if we were some kind of backward people who did not allow a girl to choose her own husband.* She could not avoid Papi's idea that the Gants were the backward ones, though, really, it was just Lester. On the duff-covered driveway, she calmed herself by considering—she scarcely knew what to call it—that sort of jealousy between the two old men. She had known of course that Papi and Lester were not cordial, but countrymen, kings on their own places, were often uncomfortable with men like themselves, happy in the company only of their own dependents. Les himself was a little like that, begrudging her the time to walk over in the afternoons to see Mami and the children, where no doubt, on account of Mami's illness, Evelyn wanted to go more often than she ought to. She was not strictly needed there. Al had married and brought his wife Hetty to live at his parents', a move generous on Hetty's part that had allowed Liesel to finish high school and marry Richard Henderson. Which Evelyn thought Liesel had a right to do, whatever Les and Papi—together in this, anyway—said about the Hendersons, who had bought land but still qualified as new to the county after ten years.

Amid the scent of her ham and potato casserole bubbling in the oven, Evelyn went into the kitchen, where Les was already filleting out catfish on the tin drainboard. She could not withhold something so disturbing as she had overheard. "I'm sorry to say, your father has taken against me."

Les had been up to fish camp to tend the throw line he ran every summer and went on making deft cuts as he listened to his wife's complaint. He had already heard from Marvin what Lester called Evelyn, and it angered him, but to hear it from her shamed him, for the underlying fact seemed to be his fault. Les had no doubt that the sterility of his marriage after three years represented his failure as a man.

The accusation that August had somehow unloaded Evelyn on the Gants was new to him, and Les seized on that. "That's unfair, we chose each other. But it's just his idea of a joke. He's a coarse old man. You want to fry this fish for dinner, or have it for supper?"

Then Evelyn was sorry she had told him in the first place—what good in it but to relieve her own feelings?—and talked about the meal they were about to eat. So they did not talk about their childlessness, and the occasion passed when she might've admitted what she had never told anybody, that, having half-raised four children already, she did not care much, except that he cared, whether they had children.

She could only, later that night, lie patiently under him when he climbed onto her and, in the onion-smelling sweat of his heartbreaking fatigue, labored with determination. Not that she disliked it, she would not have allowed herself to dislike a marital duty. When she paid more attention she could even feel—having gathered from laughing remarks among other young married women that some of them liked it—something pleasurable beginning in her, just as Les finished.

All the same, she was glad the next year when Marvin finally married blond June—in her widowed mother's fringed parlor—because the addition of another woman to the Gant family changed things. Not that Evelyn and June would be close: they were not the same kind of women, June funny and boisterous and willing to let things slide, Evelyn quiet, and in June's well-meaning word "a stickler." Really, Evelyn was strict only about her housekeeping, but people took that as meaning more about her thinking than, for good or ill, it deserved. (How to say, what point in trying, *I am not the person you take me for?*)

She was grateful for June's presence among the Gants because they stopped scrutinizing her own face in the mornings and her middle any time they felt like it and began scrutinizing June's. June conceived within a few months.

Concerning how that would be for Les, Evelyn had not thought until Marvin had come over especially to tell him. It was the fall of 1930, the cotton market had just crashed and, though the Gants were safely out of cotton by then, everybody was waiting for what would happen to beef. Then Marvin and Les were outside in that reddish-brown twilight the pine duff seemed to gather sometimes, and Evelyn could see them through the screen door but only hear Marvin say, "Sorry, *bruder*"—it seemed to be some kind of a joke—"I waited as long as I could."

Then when Les came in and told her, she understood: as if Marvin had made poor June wait four years to get married while her father died meanwhile and Marvin catted his way around the county, just so Les could have his chance at the first baby.

16

Hard times, a hobo's trained baritone sang richly and formally, *come again no more.* Evelyn picking peppers in the garden, heard that from somewhere along the river, where hobos camped to fish and nobody except old man McCoy, pacing his property with a shotgun, when he got like that, ran them off.

But the Depression did not keep the Gants from building Marvin's house, or Art's and then Chet's, soon after. Labor-rich when cash-poor, they could haul rock from the river, scrounge pipe and windows. *One of you better go get a job at the quarry or the gas fields,* Lester told his sons when men were being laid off at those places, *'cause stock farming isn't going to pay the taxes.* Men with no other choice sold their herds to the agricultural-something A. A. A., which would slaughter beef and mail you a check for not raising any more, but Lester would not sign on, and who could blame him? Cows they had bred as heifers, calves they had held darkly soaked from their mothers and had cultivated into sleek steers whose bodies they ministered to. To be slaughtered or sold for slaughter and eaten, yes: these had always been their purpose. Not

the other. *Know what they do with it? They bury it! To rot!* Hard enough that
Parker went away to join the C. C. C.—people there would think the family
was on relief; but they were not people Lester knew. To cut back on costs, the
rest of the Gant brothers worked together, field and pasture and chute, as they
had when young, and Lester paid the property taxes and bought gasoline for
tractor and truck with the money sent home from Parker's wages. The family
had food, homes.

For Evelyn, the Depression would always be Mami's dying. One close afternoon in the pines she came back from Kunkles' to find Les on the kitchen
steps bending over the small Mogul engine with which all the Gants ground
and chopped and sawed and pumped. The sun cast its shadow hugely across
the porch and onto the wall. He had not said anything against her going over
home any more since Mami had been taken so bad; Papi was the one who
made her going difficult now: she had never come soon enough or stayed long
enough.

"What is it?" Evelyn said, and Les said, "Carburetor. How is she today?"

Evelyn sat down sidewise on a step that felt hot through her skirt and
slip and leaned against the banister. "She had a good day, clear in her mind."
Les could not imagine losing either of his parents. "She said the most extraordinary thing. I had been reading to her, and she asked me if I remembered
Homecoming, 1919. That was the year Uncle Jakob found the dead woman out
at the cemetery. The dead woman in the brush arbor?"

Les remembered only that there had been such a person, one year. His
memory of homecomings was a muddle of hurried labor at the cemetery: chopping and mowing and raking and painting, in and around a rusty-fenced Gant
enclosure. Their father cared little about it except as a convenience he, or somebody, would eventually need, but its care was a civic duty he must perform. In
1919, Les had been fifteen and, from calculating that, he recalled how another
boy had told him there was a big bloody patch they could go see, but Les had
been kept too hard at work chopping weeds and bossing his brothers; probably
his father had wanted them to finish up and get back to the fields because they
didn't have school that day.

"And Mami said, 'Yes. It just came to me, she was one of the Schachner
girls.' Isn't that astonishing?"

Les had never heard of any Schachners around Iron Rock.

"No," Evelyn hadn't either. "Maybe in the cemetery." When young, Mami had known a family of that name, there had been three girls, one in her Sunday school class, but the family had moved away. "'They had that deep-browed look,' Mami said, 'with the eyes close together.'"

"A lot of people look like that."

"The very thing I remember her, or somebody, saying at the time. But something in the book I was reading to her reminded her of 'that look,' she said, and it came to her. 'It was the middle Schachner girl, with that little separation between the teeth.' She couldn't remember the girl's name."

Les did not for a moment trust what a woman who was out of her head half the time thought about a woman she had seen briefly in a coffin fifteen years before—or a girl she probably hadn't seen for fifty years. "People change a lot," he said.

"Oh but I remember that night at the church, the singing and looking at the stars, and Mami was talking to the other woman: 'I recognize that look, I just don't remember who on.' And now, maybe from having everything mixed up in her mind sometimes, she remembered. Isn't that wonderful?"

Fanciful was more like what Les thought, a Schlegel thing, or a woman's, to believe a story because they wanted to, but he did not argue with his wife, whose mother was dying. He went back to the carburetor, and the sun shone directly into Evelyn's eyes, so she got up and went into the house to start dinner.

They had been married seven years; neither of them was surprised at the other's reaction. And whether Mami had or had not identified the dead woman correctly is not the point in this story, rather that the nexus of people and times in which she lived made possible for her to think she had, and for her daughter, who lived in a comparable one, to believe her. A nexus in which, for instance, any time Evelyn was fetching or laying down potatoes or the big store beets or carrots in the root cellar—an excavation formerly half fallen-in and forgotten, now shored up by Les with new timbers—Evelyn could think of the man or men, likely enslaved, who had dug it for the ancestral Gant, who might've owned the sword they still used at the fireplace. As any time she or anybody in the four rock houses near the end of the driveway looked out through the woods towards Kunkle Road, they could be reminded of a Christmas morning in the previous century when a filly who needed no guidance had carried the body of the hanged young Gant along a rutted, dried-mud road home to the parent or parents who might have neglected a significant aspect of his up-bringing. And this memory was not confined to family or even neighbors but was public and shared with the memories of many other people who lived, or had lived, in and around Iron Rock.

After Mami died, the hearse drove out for her body and carried her back to town, where she had been born, so that, to a person who knew that, the road itself might seem to've both given and taken her life in the pines.

17

By the mid-thirties Kunkle Road, running along between the edge of the pines and the fields and pastures on the other side, was graded and graveled and, west of McCoys', continued as a paved county road towards a horizon of rough hills that on hazy days belonged to the sky. On a summer afternoon in 1936 Evelyn Gant, wearing a cotton housedress and dusty brown oxfords, trailed slowly west along the road carrying a galvanized bucket whose con-tents pressed out red juice against the bottom. The ropy scent of sun-heated fo-liage rose from the mound along the fence. The orange-red of a tanager flashed in a weave of grapevine. She had long passed Les and his brothers baling hay; off to the right lay more Gant fields, full of corn, and Gant pastures, where cattle lay down in the shade of a tree. She watched for loaded dewberry bushes, then watched, as she pulled a branch aside, for the coil of rattlesnakes that wait under them for small birds to flitter in. Amid the thorny foliage, she reached a red-stained hand and, one by one, pulled the succulent composites from thin, drying twigs and dropped handfuls into her bucket.

A hot afternoon, good for the haying. "We can get through the winter on this," Les had said. So the Gants were all right, but Evelyn had never worried about them, only about her brother Al who, now that Papi was dead too, had only Hetty and Sammy to help out—Sammy whom, grown to a fine fourteen, she hadn't seen for months, now that he had to come over to her.

She measured with her eyes the distance to McCoys' fence line; she would not pick beyond it, even on the public right-of-way. Not that anybody at Mc-Coys' would be picking dewberries this year, only that Old Man McCoy—

called *old man* for irascibility, as some men were—took offense at everything. Mrs. McCoy, who had been popular in Iron Rock, had died quite recently. *A generation is passing*, Evelyn thought, though Tessa and Lester, and Ian McCoy, were still going strong.

Al had been so rude to her since Papi's death—which had been sudden, within the year after Mami's—Evelyn seldom went over to Kunkles' anymore except for crowded family gatherings, and Sammy said Al kept him busy, which might've meant, kept him from coming to see her as often as he would've liked. If Al, who spoke against the A. A. A. but appeared to have very few cattle, had seen no choice except to sign up for it, he might've wanted to avoid inquiry. Evelyn would not have judged him. But he would not've expected her to keep such an admission from Les, which was to say, the Gants, and, as the men had to go on in that eternal necessity of neighborly relations, Al might've taken it out on her.

The sound of a vehicle approaching from the west announced a newly familiar truck, an old trembling, square-cab model, spitting gravel from beneath its tires. Evelyn stood aside in the rising dust and lifted a hand in the country way to Charlie McCoy, who was back home, let go from the stockyards in Ft. Worth. He had come home for his mother's funeral and gone right back the same day, but he had lost his job and had to come home again.

The truck skidded to a long stop and Charlie, smoking a hand-rolled cigarette, leaned out the window and yelled something that, in the loudness of the engine, Evelyn did not understand. She cupped a hand around her ear.

"—ANY GOOD?"

She held her bucket up and tipped it for him to see. He must've been on the way to town, but instead of driving on, Charlie said something else she couldn't hear. She smiled, shrugged, nodded.

"GET IN, I'll GIVE YOU A RIDE HOME."

She was not ready to go home and would never be ready to accept a ride from Charlie. The Gant brothers were friendly with Andy and him, as her own brothers of the right age had been, but she could not manage more than to feel sorry for Charlie, ill-treated as he was by his father. "Thank you, I guess I'd rather walk."

"I'M GOING RIGHT BY THERE. GET IN."

To insist on refusing made more of it than it was worth, and like his father, he would take a thing personally. She rounded the truck, climbed up next to him, and said the polite thing, "Good to have you back home."

"Not good to be back."

"I was so sorry about your mother," who people said had scraped up the money for him to leave in the first place, *to get him away from Ian*. Of another bereaved family, Evelyn would've asked, *How's everything at your place?* but she knew. *Gone to rack and ruin,* people said, meaning, *now there's nobody to stop Ian McCoy from driving it there.* Apart from the ambitious old house built by an earlier generation, McCoy's had been for years a jumble of rusty junk and tarpapered outbuildings, with Mrs. McCoy the only force for order and maintenance.

"What was it like in Ft. Worth?"

"Oh, it's a sight to see. You'n Les"—something nasty in the way Charlie said that—"ought to go up there sometime. Courthouse taller'n a steeple, brick-paved streets, and a streetcar run down Houston Street and up Main. Go to market day on the railroad platform, buy yourself a bunch of bananas from South America."

"Too bad the work ran out," Evelyn said, and that was home for you, Charlie thought, where everybody knew your business whether you wanted them to or not.

"It 'as just work." He had never liked Miss Evelyn Perfect Kunkle, and he liked her even worse as Mrs. Les Gant, Jr. That way she had, so you could just tell she was being nice to you.

Charlie'd had a woman, a former bar girl in Ft. Worth, where they lived in a one-room slope-ceilinged garage apartment and pretended to the landlord they were married. Charlie had thought of marrying her, even as he said to men who had known her before, *If milk is free, why buy a cow?* He had enjoyed the feeling of rescuing this girl, and the elimination of women as a problem in his life. He had thought of taking her someplace he would not meet men who had known her before, and his mother's death had made him wonder whether he could bring her back here, but when he returned to the apartment after the funeral, she was gone.

At the outlines of new rock houses though the pines, he slowed for the Gant driveway they were calling Gant Road now. Charlie would never've got a separate house out of his father, no matter who he'd married. "You and Les got you a good set-up. When y'all going to have you some"—Charlie said the word in the old country manner—"*chirren?*"

People had mostly stopped asking Les and Evelyn that, after nine years. Evelyn could not tell whether Charlies's asking it was merely mannerless or a sneer. "We might adopt," she said, though she knew by then they wouldn't. Thelma Heimsoth, who was married to Tessa Gant's nephew and had five children, was sick and not expected to live. *Ernst'll have a time of it without her,* Tessa said. *You could take the two youngest, if Ernst'll let them go.*

As soon as the truck stopped, she opened the door. "A orphan?" Charlie's contempt was an exaggeration of Les's incredulity: *Raise another man's children?* Who—perhaps it was for the best—would've grown up knowing their father had given them away and kept the others.

"You ought to find a nice girl yourself." Evelyn climbed down from the truck.

"Sure ain't any in Ft. Worth."

She was glad to slam the door, glad when he drove on: she hadn't endured so much of Charlie's company since they rode the old wood-sided school bus together.

Let her have, say, already washed the berries and been making berry cobbler when Les came in with the tracks of the comb showing in his dark hair. He had showered as usual in the well house and changed into clean clothes she left for him there, and he talked about the haying and his brothers. When she thought of it she said, "Charlie McCoy gave me a ride home, though I didn't want it at all."

"Did he say if Old Man McCoy means to cut his hay this year?"

"No."

"I don't know what they're going to feed, this winter if they don't. Marvin said McCoys never planted anything this year but onions."

But if Les offered Andy McCoy to come help bale hay with him if he went ahead and cut it, and Andy McCoy did that, the old man would knock him down, never mind that Andy was supposed to be the favorite. Andy could not cut hay until the old man took a notion to do some work, as in the spring when they had castrated a few calves and planted the kitchen garden solid in onions; and if the old man never took a notion, the hay would have to rot in the field.

Ian McCoy was not quite crazy, but he had always been incomprehensible to his neighbors, and his wife's death seemed to have removed the last practical constraints on his behavior. Maybe he was only willful in despite of anybody, including himself. He brought lawsuits he was certain to lose. When he finished a job or stopped working, he threw his tools on the ground and left them, so the next time he wanted them, he had to remember, where is my augur, where is my sharp-shooter, and they probably would've rusted. Once, shortly after he had inherited the property, he had done the unthinkable: he had sold land. Not forced to do so, having taken out a mortgage for a tractor or a family emergency and gotten caught by markets or weather. *He sold land and lived on the money.* A man like that was almost beyond worrying about.

"Go up to fish camp and run my throw line tomorrow morning," Les told Evelyn. *My lazy man's trot line,* he called it, because he did not have to swim or get in a boat to tend it. "'Cause I never got there today, and I'm not going to, tomorrow."

She had often done that in other summers. Fish was a relief from home-canned or -salted meat. Unless they killed an animal, they had fresh only if somebody had an errand worth burning the gasoline for and could stop by the locker in town.

18

For Evelyn to enter the sharper scent of hot pine at mid-day with Les's canvas fishing bag over her shoulder was to distance tractor growl and enter an irregular sound shape of layered insect buzz; to engage with the sticky guy-wires and scrim of spider art; to rediscover, in the thick streaky light, a storage annex to her mind. She came suddenly on a memory not thought of for years, of another trail, the one to Kunkles': when she was a small child, a storm had blown a big dead tree half down across it, and Papi and Gus and Fred had cut off enough of the bottom to reopen the trail, but the rest had hung there alongside it for years, reaching into the tops of other trees and, in later storms, coming down in big pieces. She recalled problems at different times of climbing over or removing its wood. So at the first moment when she came out into the clearing at fish camp, the empty pilings in the river surprised her, as if she had not known that the pier was washed away in the spring flood.

The sight of Charlie McCoy sprawled on the bank fishing brought her all too sharply back to the present. She greeted him and inquired of his fishing in the neighborly way.

"Doughbait," he said, "though I might ought to catch me some bait perch."

Did he say that so she would offer, "Take some from the trap?"—Les's wire trap a dozen yards or so downstream, which he surely knew about.

"Nah," Charlie said. Not even, *But thanks,* though surely Inge had tried.

In the shack, Evelyn pulled on Les's waders, rolled her skirt up and tied it down over their tops. She scuffed awkwardly in them to the bank, where she again had to say something. "And how's everybody at your-all's place?"

"He shuts himself up in his room" —as if there was only one *he* at that house—"reading *The Saturday Evening Post.*"

When she clambered down the bank, the water, low now, was only thigh-high. She wallowed alongshore to the fish trap, pulled it up and thrust a hand in among the flopping shine of small perch. One by one—*Two to lose*—she dropped five into her bag.

Farther downstream at the tree where Les tied the line, she hauled at its heaviness: the rock anchor, if nothing more. The first drop line came up half-floating; the second came up snarled, where something had twisted free; but the third was taut.

"You got you a fish," Charlie said from the bank, right before an armored reptilian ancient-looking creature—"Garfish, too bad"—broke the water. It looked dead. "Don't try to unhook it. Cut it loose and let it go." Evelyn did not need Charlie McCoy's advice. "You can beat one of them things to death, and fifteen minutes later it'll wake up and bite you."

It was dead and smelled like decaying water weeds as she worked it loose. She flung it up on the bank. "I can split it open for the chickens."

"With a axe, you can." *Yes, Charlie, with an axe.*

Evelyn rebaited the drop lines and, with both hands, heaved the rock anchor as far out into the river as she could, where it fell with a *glunk*. The current would pull the drop lines into the deep hole.

"Sure miss a woman around our place. Had a girl in Ft. Worth that I wish I never met. I gave her everything a woman could want, and when I went back after Mama's funeral, she was gone. Skedaddled. Never left so much as a note."

"That was bad of her."

"She was a evil woman."

"Maybe you'll find yourself a nice girl around here." Evelyn supposed there were girls who would feel fortunate to marry a McCoy, even Charlie.

"Andy could find hisself one."

Evelyn waded back up to the low place to climb out and Charlie said—the presumption!—"You and me could've got married."

Evelyn said, "Or you and Lou Larrimer," which she knew was unkind.

"Shoot, Lou Larrimer wouldn't've looked at me if I was made of gold."

Back at the house when Les came in, she said, "Nothing but a dead gar and Charlie McCoy."

"He's been up there a lot," Les said. "Reckon he likes to stay away from his old man."

"He said his father shuts himself up in his bedroom and reads *The Saturday Evening Post* all day."

Les thought, not for the first time in his life, that was a helluva father to have.

19

The next time Les asked Evelyn to run the throw line, her first pleasure at the thought of fish camp was spoiled by the next one, of Charlie, until she remembered he would not be there that day. Old Man McCoy had finally taken a notion to cut his hay, it was now dried, and the Gant brothers were going to help Andy and Charlie bale it. In the morning kitchen, Evelyn finished straining the new milk, scalding the milking utensils, mixing the old milk with rennet to make the cottage cheese they called *smearkase*. Then she set out in the freshness on the spongy, sun-streaked trail amid the *oo-OOH* of doves and the single, repeated tambourine *chink* of a tiny yellow bird she knew no name for. She watched high up for the big woodpecker with the red topknot that flew with slow wingbeats like a crow. Farther on, crows flapped and called in the treetops, their complaints loudening at a place where they seemed to dive and rise overhead and dive again. She angled to see up though the branches until something big and mottled brown that would be a hawk they'd mobbed rose and sailed slowly off.

When she came out into the moving air of the clearing, she was surprised to see Charlie McCoy sitting on the riverbank as before, leaning against a tree under the crooked fringe of pine needles a frail branch held out over his head. He held a fishing rod but did not seem to hear her. Maybe he was asleep. He ought to be ashamed to be caught here, Evelyn thought, with the neighbors out haying his father's field.

She went on into the dusty screenwire shack, and the slam of the spring-less door might have wakened him because he called, "Who's that?" You could not see into the screenwire except at just the right angle, and he did not get up. Evelyn tapped Les's waders against the bench to knock out any spiders or scorpions.

When she clomped out of the shack in the waders with the stained canvas fishing bag over her shoulder, he said, "Oh, it's you." His casualness rang false, giving her the distasteful impression that he was there in hopes that she would be.

"I thought they were haying over at your place today," she said.

"Andy and the old man are. Their work."

This blasphemy against the family compact, *your home, your labor*, shocked her. "I would've thought it belonged to all of you." *Your labor, your land.*

"Ain't no part of mine. The old man left it to Andy."

Across under the pines, the water was green glass, and what he said seemed impossible. But he was speaking of Ian McCoy.

"He did, wrote out a new will after Mama died and flat-out disinherited me. I seen it at the bank, left everything to Andy."

"I'm so sorry." She climbed down the slope and splashed in. "Why?"

"Why does he do anything?'

She apprehended the injustice of being Ian McCoy's son. "It seems terribly unfair."

"Andy 'as real big about it, says I can live there long as I want. But I dang well ain't working for him."

She attempted lightness. "So you fish."

"Keep the old man from saying, 'What, you eatin' again?'"

"Does he really say that?"

"Sure he does, said it all my life."

The swish of the stained canvas bag said, *poor Charlie, poor Charlie.* Perch from the trap wriggled rainbows in the sun.

When Evelyn hauled in the rock anchor, the first drop line floated up, but the second, from the deep hole, was taut. She pulled it in slowly. Just before the fish broke a sudden swirl of water, Charlie shouted from the bank, "It's a yaller cat!"

Not likely—years since Evelyn had seen an opelousa from that river— but it was, the shovel skull, the mottled yellowish skin unmistakable. Les would be pleased: it must be twelve or thirteen pounds, enough to share out in the family as a small reward for a day helping the neighbors.

"Lemme help you," Charlie said. He rummaged with the butt of his fishing rod among clattering rocks in a pile under the tree.

"I don't need help, Charlie, but thank you."

"Sure you do."

In the shallows the yellow heaved feebly. Avoiding the fins, the feelers with their look of a handlebar mustache, Evelyn sought a grip on the scaleless skin, thrust the fingers of one hand into a gill and reached with the other into her bag. The heavy fish twitched, then hung exhausted from her hand.

Charlie splashed down and waded towards her, disturbing the water as she worked with rusty pliers at the hook in the out-thrust jaw.

A leg in jeans wet to the knee, nudged alongside her in the water. His hand reached for the pliers—"Charlie!" She held onto the fish, pulled the pliers away from him.

He grabbed them, ripping the hook through the lip of the fish, which wrenched itself sidewise out of her grip and leaped into the shallows, where it paused with feelers moving in the water. "I got it," Charlie said and it swished away between his hands.

"Oh, Charlie. Look what you've done."

He was sorry, he was sorry, holding up his hands as if to mean no more harm, and sloshed towards the bank, where he slipped—"Shit"—and fell forward. "I'm sorry, I'm sorry, I can't even talk right around a woman."

She re-baited the hook—all she could do—and the others, and heaved the rock out as hard as if she'd been throwing it at Charlie. At the climb-out he sat with cow-licked head in hands, and she remembered disliking the cap-shaped back of his head when they were at school, which had surely been unfair of her. Above her, his face was wet. Could he possibly have been crying? "I can't do nothing right," he moaned, "I ain't got nothing, and I ain't never going to have."

At the likely truth of these claims, she forgave him. "It's just a fish, Charlie." Instead of climbing the bank, she went over to where he sat and touched his arm. "You can give us one when you catch it."

He wiped his face with a hand, leaving streaks of mud. "Don't tell Les."

"Oh, Charlie."

"Promise me you won't."

This demand both embarrassed and annoyed her because she had meant to. She assured him she wouldn't, and he reached for her, and she held him off in the upper-arm-clutch of the not-close at funerals. He pulled her towards him as if it had been another kind of embrace and she pulled away and began to climb the bank.

"Well," he said, as if something had happened between them, but he had to be pretending.

In the shack Evelyn pulled off the wet waders and regretted having promised not to tell Les, because, without the part about the fish, she could not explain why she had made a sympathetic gesture to Charlie and how he had pretended to mistake it.

As she walked back through a late-morning wood silent of birds except for crows, trouble seemed to surround the thought of Charlie McCoy, as if he made it from everything that did not make it for him. Then she thought it was just as well not to tell Les about the fish, it would only disappoint him.

"Nothing on the lines," she said when Les came in hot, tired, and dirty at dinnertime.

"Shucks, had my mouth all set for fish."

"Charlie was there again."

"He sure wasn't out haying. I asked Andy if Charlie was coming, and he said no. Some kind of falling out over there."

"Charlie said the old man disinherited him after his mother died, left the whole place to Andy."

"You don't say. What'd Charlie do to bring that on himself?"

"According to him, nothing. After Inge died, Ian apparently wrote a new will and just wrote him out of it, for no reason."

"Sounds about right."

"But Les." Then all she could say was what seemed to come from nowhere: "The trouble with Charlie McCoy is, he wants too much from you when you talk to him."

"Aw, he's a good old boy," Les said, and Evelyn wondered yet again what men meant when they used that expression about another man.

20

Charlie, who had trailed along with the Gant brothers as a kid without ever being a friend of any one of them, was also distantly related to them, in the way that many people around Iron Rock were to each other: his mother Inge had been a Biedermann, and a Biedermann of her generation had married a Heimsoth. When Tessa Heimsoth Gant had heard about Charlie's absence from the haying, she said, "That boy needs a good talking to."

Give her a wooden chair in the corn shuckers' circle at one end of her crowded kitchen, where Les, resting arm and shoulder from his turn on the scraper, stripping cob after cob of kernels and milk, had told Charlie's story about Old Man McCoy's will. In the circle sat bushel baskets from the field heaped with the rough sheathed ears, galvanized buckets filling with the shiny, kerneled cobs of corn, and other buckets filling with shucks or scraped cobs. At the cookstove-and-drainboard end of the kitchen, a many-armed contrivance of adults scraped cobs, sluiced the pulp into big pots, stirred it attentively as it boiled into thick bubbles, and, from kettles of boiling water, scalded quart Mason jars to receive it, new rings and lids to secure it.

Tessa got up to take a turn at the hot work. "Ian never would've done such a thing, if Inge had lived."

Beginning to ladle creamed corn into the wide-mouth glass funnel, moving it with a rag from jar to jar, where any splash was a burn, any sudden move a blister, Tessa thought how true it was that a woman's fate and that of her children was determined by the man she married. June followed her along the row of jars, wiping their lips with a steaming wet rag; Evelyn followed June, screwing down rings with a fresh towel and setting each jar on the rack in the next pressure cooker, which already waited on the stove. Each daughter-in-law had brought her own, along with her tea-kettle and the segmented cardboard boxes where the jars had accumulated as they were emptied over the winter.

When Tessa sat down to shuck again, she said, "I miss Inge's garden," because no one could think about Inge McCoy without remembering her flower garden. It had run along one side of the house, and though Old Man McCoy had been a trial to his wife in the ways widely known and spoke roughly to her besides, he had ploughed it for her, early every spring, running furrows carefully around her rose-of-Sharon and japonica and bridal wreath and gardenia, and the places where her daisies and peonies and chrysanthemums would come up again. Amid everything else she did, she would find time to divide the dahlia and iris tubers, spread rotted chicken manure on the glads and irises, and sow the empty furrows with seed rubbed from the previous year's dried flower-heads, stock, larkspur, hollyhock, marigold.

"I suppose that's gone to ruin, too," Tessa said, and Les said everything had that hadn't already.

Later he carried out buckets of corncobs to Marvin's pigs and, remembering while he was out, *A change is as good as a rest,* walked on up to fish camp to run his line. Charlie was there as usual and, passing the time of day in the usual way, Les felt sorry for him about the will but did not, of course, say anything. A man did not want you to feel sorry for him.

21

The day after Sammy had been up to see Evelyn, Les said to her, "Run that throw line for me this afternoon, would you?" The Gant brothers were grinding sorghum for cattle cake and the whole settlement of Gant houses smelled like pine-flavored molasses; then the gasoline well-pump had gone out, adding a sick-making burnt smell. As Les was the best mechanic among them, repairs always fell to him.

Evelyn was canning tomatoes in their own hot kitchen. She said, "I wish there was somebody else to send. Buster"—Marvin's boy—"is too little. Too bad Sammy didn't come today instead of yesterday."

"You mean 'cause I don't have a boy of my own to send?"

"No, Les Gant, I do not mean that."

He went back out again without saying anything, and she knew he was just harried and would make up for it later by speaking extra nicely to her. Presently she would obey him like a good wife, as she should've done to begin with. All the same, she remembered the pain of Sammy's still calling her his *Mamichen*. She was not, she was Les Gant's wife, as she meant to be, only she had not thought she would have to choose.

Along the river the sun-heated air held in by the pines was released slowly to rise in an updraft where, high up over one bank, turkey vultures teetered, hunting by smell and saving the energy flying took. Charlie sprawled under his usual tree and watched them for a while. When he looked down again at the bobber he could not stare at because it put him to sleep, a motion across the river caught his eye. Then he watched a squirrel on the sterile ground under the trees busying itself over an old cone. If he'd had his rifle, he could've hit the little sucker easy. He could've found out, too, whether a bump on a tree trunk he had studied, where a limb grew out, was a roosting owl or just a bump on a tree. His afternoon seemed thickly coated, immobilized.

The arrival of Evelyn in the clearing in her housedress with Les Gant's canvas bag over her shoulder, reminded Charlie of everything he would never have. He sat up and called, "Where you been?"

She might've given him a funny look before she went into the shack, and he thought how fickle women were, how sympathetic they could seem without it being anything to do with you.

She came out to the bank in the waders, and he said "What's the matter with you?" He didn't even know what he was doing with her, just something.

"How're you today, Charlie?"

"I kept a big catfish alive for you, 'til it was fixing to die."

"You could've given it to Les."

He stuck out a hand to help her down the bank but she wouldn't take it. "You told him."

"That you lost his fish? No. I told him your father cut you out of his will, and Les was terribly sorry to hear that." She waded along the shore to the trap: conversation ended, that's it for you, buddy.

"I used to like Les," Charlie said louder, "'til he took to helping Andy out. And you can tell him that, too."

She looked back at him over her shoulder and said, in that woman's way of tidying up after something you'd said, "Mrs. McCoy always did so much for everybody. Tessa was remembering her flower garden not long ago."

"Gone to weed and seed."

"Maybe you could bring it back in her memory."

"You're gooder'n Andy at thinking up things for me to do."

Evelyn sloshed on upstream, aware of Charlie's gaze, and bent to the trap, remembering him at school, that air of resentment, as if his misfortune might be your fault and you owed him for it.

When she hauled in the line, Charlie, who had stood up so he could see before she could whether there was anything on it, called, "Ya'll got all the luck."

That turned out to be about the chucklehead on the last drop line, which was probably muddy-tasting, but he might not have been able to see what it was. She considered letting it go: it must've been two pounds and would feed the chickens if Les didn't want it. She dropped it into the bag.

She wished, as she re-baited the hooks and turned back towards the climb-out that she needn't even be polite to such an offensive neighbor. "Outside of fishing," she said, "I guess you have to make your own luck."

"Shoot, I ain't never had a chance."

"Still do. What'd you want to be in high school?"

"A cowboy on a trail drive. Why I went to work at the stockyards."

That work was all gone now. She swung Les's bag up onto the bank. "There must be other things you know how to do."

"Fishin' and squirrel huntin'. I can blast 'em out of the tree at fifty yards, but they ain't any pay in that."

"Maybe you could get on at the C. C. C., like Parker."

"Uh, uh, not me, feller. I ain't running a shovel for nobody."

And that, in a phrase, seemed like what was wrong with Charlie McCoy—and his father, too. "Oh, Charlie."

As if she had said it in some completely different way, he held both arms down to her. She avoided them and climbed the bank, but he caught her by the waist when she neared the top. "I'm a hopeless, son-of-a-gun, Mrs. Les Gant, and you can't say it away," and pulled her to him.

"Charlie!" He buried his face in the open collar of her dress and she shoved herself away from him. "I'm surprised at you."

"I'm just foolin'." He released her slowly, his hands lingering, and as he pulled them away, a thumb grazed her bosom.

She got to her feet—"Well, don't fool with me"—and snatched up her sack.

She was mad, and when she had scuffed to the shack and left off Les's waders, she bypassed the entrance to the woods trail and took Fish Camp Road the long way home, because she was mad at Les in advance. She would tell him, *He swung me up and touched my bosom, whether he meant to or not,* and Les would say, *I reckon he didn't mean to,* or some excuseful rubbish.

When she got home, he was in the kitchen and still hadn't been able to get the well-pump running, and it was too late to disconnect the Mogul from the unfinished grinding job and rig it up to the pump. The Gant family had just as much water for stock tanks as they might choose to drain from their elevated household cisterns. Les, beyond irritation, had settled into the fatal-ism of farmers: *Ain't one thing, it's another.* "Have to drive 'em to the river."

Still, she had to tell him something. "That Charlie McCoy was grabbing at me."

"Reckon he was just horsing around." It seemed both true and not quite. In neat strokes with his filleting knife, Les stripped out the fish and laid the meat on the tin drain board.

22

In the solitary, birdsong mornings after Les had left for field or pasture Evelyn, at her own work around house and yard, tried to guess from what she knew of his work whether he might come in for their noon dinner already knowing he could do no more than finish what he was doing before dark and would ask her to go run his line. Sometimes in the afternoons she got out of the way, up to June's or Tessa's on some errand, so if he came in for a glass of cold tea and to ask her that, he would do it himself. She did not like shirking, adding to his work: she was to be his helpmeet.

One morning she was in the dim, still-cool kitchen when Les, who was supposed to be harvesting cowpeas with the rest of the Gants, carried a bloody feed sack into the yard, the two dogs dancing and whining around him. "Stay," he commanded, and the door slammed.

The sack held a quarter of beef. "Bloody," he said, because the animal had struggled, "but not too." A Gant steer had crossed a Kunkle fence, fallen into a draw, and broken its leg. Al Kunkle had found it by the circling buzzards and shot it, and Gants had known what it was, though not whose, from the buzzards and that single shot.

By the time Les and Chet got there, Al and Sammy were skinning out the carcass with long smooth strokes of the knife, and the four of them butchered it together. That was the kind of time when you needed those good neighborly relations: there was no discussion over the condition of the fence or who was responsible; they divided the meat equally between the two families—Les and Chet dividing the Gants' between them—and left the rest for the dogs and the birds.

"And there's half the morning gone," Les complained to Evelyn, "and the meat to take to the locker"—all except a big steak he wanted for dinner.

"I'll do it," she said quickly, but he still said, "and will you run my throw line afterwards? 'Cause I'm never going to get to it now."

When she got back from town, she drove on up to Marvin and June's house, hoping to find Buster, who was five, to walk along with her, but the wind had come up, the soughing of the pines was a groan, and the house lay empty, the long, light bedroom curtains blowing out unscreened windows on one side. June and the children were probably at Tessa's, but to go up there wanting Buster to go to fish camp with her would seem like too much, and she would have to explain.

Evelyn thought of driving around to fish camp—why did that feel better?—then would not waste the gas. On the trail, she hoped Charlie might not be there, but he was. Not to sound as irritable as she felt, she did not speak to him when he greeted her arrival, as if she might not have heard him in the breeze-loud woods.

When she came out of the fish shack, he said, "What's eating you?" as if she had been a troublesome girlfriend.

"Charlie, you have no right to speak to me that way." She avoided the bank where he sprawled, chose instead an awkwardly higher place a little downriver and eased down to sit, holding the waders on as her feet dangled.

"Aw, now, you don't have to do that," he said.

She held her skirt down where she had tied it and half-slid, half-jumped into the water. But she would not be able to climb back up that way.

"Like I'm a rabid dog," he said. She bent to the fish trap, bright perch that escaped her hand only briefly.

As she waded downstream, he called, "It ain't like I'm going to hurt you."

She knew that was true. She hauled in the line, watching the murk rise in the water from the rock scraping up mud across the bottom. A waste of time and effort for nothing except snarled drop-lines, one hook missing, two empty of even scraps of perch. She replaced and rebaited.

When she went back towards the only stretch of bank she could climb in the waders, where Charlie sat, she said, "Charlie, I have to pass by you, and I'm going to ask you to keep your hands to yourself."

He stood up and put them behind his back. "Yes, teacher."

Though he kept them there as she climbed up, he pled like a lover, "Just lemme touch you. Your arm, your shoulder, you don't know how long it's been since I touched a woman."

"That," she said, "is nothing to do with me." She tried to pass by him quickly, but he feinted at her with his hands, blocking her way, and she slapped at them as she went, then hated the gesture, because it seemed flirtatious. "I'm going to tell Les."

"Ooh," he said, "big bad Les Gant. And I'll tell him you like it."

At a safe distance, she turned to face him. "If you do, you will bear false witness against me." The disturbance of the pines made it seem as if had already done so.

When Les came in, freshly showered from the well house, she was frying more steak in the kitchen and said without turning around, "Charlie McCoy made improper advances to me."

She felt his skeptical look. "What'd he do now?'

"He kept trying to touch me, or he pretended he was."

"He was just fooling."

"I don't care what he was doing, he behaved improperly."

"Charlie McCoy's never behaved properly in his life. He's a dang fool, and I get embarrassed for him."

"He pretended like he was going to touch my bosom."

"Well, it's a kid thing to do, and somebody ought to taught him better." Les had a vague feeling of failure, as if he himself ought to've.

"He said he used to like you 'til you started helping Andy out."

Les laughed. "Did he? Now that's a thing a person could like about Charlie, that he'll say what Andy's just thinking. A man doesn't necessarily like you for helping him, even if he needs it."

23

Almost as much as having to bat Charlie McCoy's hands away from her, Evelyn hated what his behavior had done to fish camp. A place, as Sammy had said after Papi died, was like nothing else. Their oldest brother August and his wife Anna, who had reared their family already, had offered to take Bea and Sammy so they did not have to go so far to school, and Sammy was trying to explain why he had declined. "If it was just the people, I might've done it. I don't hardly know Gus," who had been gone before Sammy was born, "but I might've tried him out. Al's a hard man, and we get crosswise sometimes.

"But with Al and Hetty and them"—their three small children—"I stay *here,* and a place is like nothing else. You know that big live oak in the middle of the east pasture? To anybody else it's just a tree where cows lay down."

"*Lie* down," she said, because she had let him get away with one, and Sammy smiled as if he had said it on purpose.

"To me that's the place where the cow was calving when I was seven, the first one they let me watch, only it was coming out wrong, and Papi and Al were going to send me back to the house. Then Papi reached in with a rope— I'd never seen anything like that before, right into the cow—and he and Al put the rope over their shoulder and pulled, and the cow bellowed, and there was the calf all wet on the ground, dragged into the world by the rope around its back feet. I remember that when I look at that tree. Places are the holders of memories."

I give Evelyn, musing over this memory of a conversation about memories, to be slicing enormous red tomatoes, the purple onions Les liked raw, for an easy salad in the endless train of meals prepared. When she thought of fish camp now, of being proposed to there—how cool Les's lips were when he kissed her—or of the first small perch she caught there on a cane pole, or of learning to swim as a child there—*Put your face in the water and blow bub-*

bles, Kurt told her—those memories seemed overlaid with a greasy residue of resentful Charlie McCoy. She supposed she ought not to take his behavior personally: she could not see what harm he could do her.

And even if that last line—foreshadowing? dramatic irony?—seems obvious, it makes an opportunity for me to say that, contrary to appearances in, for instance, my story's opening allusions to a crime and the now-rising action between Evelyn and Charlie, her story is not about rape. She will not have been raped; if she believed she had, the outcome for her might be quite different. I make this point because there are too many rape stories—and when I say that, I am not speaking of the necessary witness that sanity and justice require following an actual rape, I am speaking only of what seems possible for me now in fiction.

With that said, perhaps I may risk another foreshadowing: I give Evelyn to remember the summer Kurt was teaching her to swim, when he seized her shoulder and pointed to the swimming V of a water moccasin: *If you see that V coming towards you, dive deep, 'cause those things'll come after you and bite you in the water.*

24

She was already washing dinner dishes the next time Les asked her to go run his line for him, and she had thought out in advance what she would say. She turned with a shiny pot lid in her hand, and a spot of sunlight bounced around the kitchen like the memory of her own thought. At the sitting end of the big kitchen Les was headed for the camelback chair where he took a half-hour nap before he went back to work for the afternoon. She said, "I'm sorry, Les Gant, but I cannot go up there. Let me do something else to help you." It was the first time in their marriage she had ever directly refused him anything.

"There's no reason for that. It's just Charlie McCoy."

"There is. I'm almost afraid of him."

Les sat down heavily in the chair: the heat, more than the work, exhausted him. Even if Charlie hadn't been harmless—and dammit, that was what was wrong with him—he would never harm a Gant. He wouldn't dare.

"As long as he is likely to be up there, I cannot go."

Les threw up his hands in a gesture his father used about his mother, *Dutch-stubborn;* he could tell she would not be argued out of it this time. He heaved himself back up out of the chair and went out on the back porch to fetch his canvas fishing bag. Now he would be tired the rest of the day because his wife had taken a notion against a pathetic s. o. b. he knew better than she did.

In the close woods, which were at least shady, though only a different hot from the blazing pea-field, Les went on thinking about the cowardice of Charlie, who should've clocked Old Man McCoy when he got big enough. One time would've done it if he'd said the right thing. Instead he let the old man go on talking him down to his face and he himself had gone on being mad at the world. But walking amid the churchly columns of the pines in the heat-strong smell that had always been the smell of freedom, Les calmed down and supposed he might resign himself to running the line if it got done. He wondered how important the principle involved was.

Charlie as usual lolled on the bank, and Les glimpsed an alien charm in having nothing. "A good afternoon to take off," he said, and Charlie poormouthed about not having nothing requiring his attention, which made the exchange about how much Les himself had, or would have.

In the fish shack pulling on his waders, he wondered whether Charlie had to tease Evelyn because he had no wife of his own and had to live in the same house with his father and would inherit nothing, unless he changed his mind again. Those things counted more with some men than with others.

When Les came out in his waders, he said, "You know, Charlie, my wife's German, like your mother and mine, and those folks can be a little limited in their sense of humor. Reckon you ought not to joke around with her 'cause she gets her feelings hurt."

"Shoot," Charlie said. "I was just funning with her. I never meant no harm."

"I reckon you didn't, Charlie. Just trying to keep the peace at home." They laughed.

The throw line was so heavy when Les pulled on it, it might've caught a snag until the pulse was too strong to be the current; then it might have been the big channel cat Les had glimpsed once that summer rising like an ambition in the deep hole. He pulled steadily, easily, but the line gave two desperate jerks and went slack. He'd lost it, whatever it had been. On the first drop, there was nothing, not even the hook, and he felt around carefully in the pocket of the bag for another one. On the second drop, there was nothing but the hook; on the third—he saw the shape of the head as it came up—a small blue cat, but big enough to keep.

Charlie, who had done even better, showed off his own catch, and Les was glad for him and headed home with the satisfaction of wild meat: every wild creature you could eat helped make one less of your own you had to. On the woods trail, he suspected that to indulge his wife farther might represent a failure on his part. She was to be his helpmeet, and if it came down to it, a man ought to be able to control his wife. He would not invent an occasion to assert his authority, but the next time he absolutely had to have her help at fish camp, he would have it, by God, and she would understand why.

When he carried his catch into the house, she had already cleaned up from dinner and sat in her rocking chair by the cold fireplace darning one of his socks. Out of respect for her clean kitchen and consideration for what he had resolved to do, he took the fish back outside to butcher.

But, as it happened, the next time Les meant to ask for her help, Sammy had stopped by in the truck because Al had to send somebody to town, and Les could make a joke of needing for Evelyn to go to fish camp: "If y'all are going to be jawing for awhile, drive up to fish camp for me and run my throw line, would you?"

Sammy was pleased to drive anywhere and especially to drive Evelyn. In the Kunkle truck he talked about the stile he had built in the wire fence between Kunkles' and Gants' "so we don't have to climb the fence anymore." This seemed sad to Evelyn since she went to Kunkles' so seldom now and none of them except Sammy came to her house—Bea never, engaged and, as it were, already gone into her own world. But Sammy would use the new stile, might even have built it wishing that his *Mamichen* came more often, so it was about his love of her, and she tried to look at it that way.

At fish camp, where Charlie had squinted around the tree at the sound of the truck, Sammy said he would run Les's line and went into the shack for the waders. Then Evelyn stood outside talking to Sammy through the screen so it wouldn't look like she was just avoiding Charlie. But when Sammy came out in the waders and he and Evelyn crossed to the climb-down, he had to talk to Charlie, who made him admit he had a trot-line all the way across the river and a little wooden skiff—"Papi built it"—to tend it from.

Charlie said, "I wish somebody'd ever built me a little skiff to tend a trotline from." Sammy splashed down the bank into the shallows. "Reckon you come down in the world, wade around in the muck running Les Gant's line."

Along the high bank, Evelyn walked downriver following Sammy.

Les was back in the sun cutting cornstalks with the others, where maybe his unresolved grievance with Evelyn hardened in him like a clod, because in the days after, he began to feel that she had failed him where he had a right to rely on her. Small things other family members neglected or inequitably left to him exasperated him, and he raised his voice to them, as rarely. June remarked on it to Evelyn, asking if he was quite well, but Evelyn said, "I think he's just irritable in the heat." To have told her, even in confidence, that she and Les had disagreed about something trivial, would have seemed to Evelyn both silly and disloyal.

The afternoon the Gants were doing a second poor cutting of their east hayfield, a part on the baler broke, and Les worked on it until dark but could not get it fixed. He came into the kitchen annoyed at suppertime: he would have to get up before daylight and drive to Sears and Roebuck in San Antonio to be there when they opened, would have to spend precious family cash on the part, "And we'll still lose half a day."

"Tomorrow," he said fiercely to Evelyn, "you will have to run the throw line yourself, and I don't want to hear a word from you against it." She sat silent, battered by his words, and could imagine no end to the situation except Charlie's going away again.

But, for this time, as soon as Les was gone in the morning, she walked the damp pine straw through still-silent woods as the light came up slowly. A spotted brown butterfly, wings laid together, clung to a tree trunk; a mockingbird whistled in a tentative way. When Evelyn had put on Les's waders and stood on the bank, the shoreline up and down the river was still mantled by a blue-gray haze, the smooth surface of the water as dull-colored as on a winter day. She climbed down past the tackle box that was at least closed, seeing small tracks around it as if something—a raccoon?—had tried to get into it: maybe the smell of stinkbait.

In the instant before she disturbed the surface of the water, it became abruptly a mirror. A largish long-legged bird she had not seen rose from the far shore and startled up a pair of kildees that flew crying. They all had seen the sunrise at the same moment, ordinary to them—she waded downstream—a small gift to her. On the throw-line Evelyn hauled in a rabbit-faced channel cat, tasty eating and big enough to share. She walked home through the morning whistle of birds, feeling prosperous and free and determined not to mind Charlie McCoy whatever he did.

25

Charlie, after discarding jeans and week-stained under-drawers to swim, lolled naked on the bank in the hot afternoon. If people came into the clearing he could holler at them to hold up while he got decent, but if it was Evelyn, he would let her see him. He aired out the family jewels, opened his legs and rubbed at his peter roughly and thought of things he would like to do to her. Take that, for whatever she had told Les, who thought he could tell a man who to joke with and was always big Les Gant when he talked to you and you were little Charlie McCoy. And always would be in this place.

As often, Charlie thought of getting out of here, hitting the road, becoming a hobo if nothing better. He had even fancied a way to make himself go: shoot Andy or his father, or both of them; then he would have to head for Mexico, and maybe he could live there somehow. So what if he got caught on the way, he told himself, and ended up in the electric chair, how much would he have lost? In a breeze that rocked the branches overhead, sun and shade washed back and forth across his skin, and he thought of lying in a hammock in Mexico, and his mind ambled towards sleep.

Then he had actually been asleep and sat up with a blue-veiner in his hand as Evelyn Gant, who had not yet seen him, headed across the clearing. She stopped and stood with her mouth open, and a squirrel on the ground stopped, tail in the air, as if mocking her. "Yep," Charlie called out, "that's just what you think it is."

Evelyn, who in spite of being prepared to encounter Charlie had seen in the first moment only a naked man on the bank, had to look at his face to recognize him. Holding that part of himself, Charlie gestured towards her with it. "Want to touch it?"

Unstrung, she laughed and stood there for another moment before she turned around and re-crossed the clearing the way she had come. Why would he say that? Stepping quickly along the spongy trail again brought her, after some distance, back to herself and she wished she had not laughed. For a moment she could wonder if the strange encounter had really happened—except that, if it hadn't, she would have gone on across the clearing to the shack as she had intended, would've put on the waders, and climbed down to run the line.

On the bank, Charlie sat astonished at what he had done, more satisfied than not. The trees had already begun to gather dimness under them, the river gave back the reflection of their green, and a blue jay flew away, the white on its wings startling in that world of brown and green. *Time to go,* Charlie thought vaguely, congratulating himself on not caring what Les Gant or anybody else said—or did. He supposed he might have just succeeded in burning up his life here without shooting anybody, might've found as good a way as any to drive himself away from the place. At the thought, he got up and pulled on his clothes. If Les came to the house, where the old man might be out with a shotgun at the sound of a stranger, Charlie would have to call him off. Then he would go out to Les and they would talk like kings on a battlefield about what Charlie might or might not have done.

26

When Les came in from the well-house in clean clothes and his wife started in about Charlie, his first thought was that she had ceased to be rational on the subject. The claim, ". . . lying on the bank, *fooling with his privates!*" caught him in mid-step as if he himself had been guilty of something.

He said stupidly, "Well, he ought not to," and went on across the kitchen and stood by the cold fireplace looking at the eight-day clock on the mantel, which he wound every Sunday. For a moment he wondered if the boy could be deliberately baiting her; she was the kind of, what they used to call, strait-laced woman a certain kind of man, boy, really, might do that to. The idea that cringing Charlie, after being asked to tone down the joking, might have ramped it up seemed so outrageous Les looked for a more practical explanation. "Sounds like you surprised him at a private moment."

Evelyn, who had steadied her nerves by wrapping a bleached floursack apron around her still-slim middle and laying out the Blue Willow plates for a cold supper, was confounded by this remark: Les seemed unable, or unwilling, to see except through Charlie's eyes. For a moment, she did not know what to say.

"Les, he *said* something to me!"

". . ?"

"He asked me if I wanted to touch it!"

No he didn't, Les thought, he had just seen her make that up, after he wouldn't take her seriously enough. She seemed out of control here and, re-calling her novel-reading, Schlegel turn of mind, he wondered if she could be getting loony from not having children, as some women were said to do. "You must've misunderstood him."

"I did not misunderstand." And here I as author, creator and created in language, observe that Evelyn did not know the words to say clearly, *he had an erection* or *he was sexually aroused*. Her husband's unwillingness to believe what she had seen astonished her. She supposed if he wouldn't stand up for her, he would have to stand up for the proprieties.

"Charlie McCoy was naked on the bank in a place where anybody of your family or mine might come. What if I had taken Dilly," Marvin's four-year-old Delia, "with me?"

It was the single reasonable objection Les could discover in his wife's re-sponse to what might've been a natural enough circumstance, and he was glad to fix on it. "I'll speak to him about that."

Evelyn left it. Later she wondered what she had expected: all the Gant brothers were like that, closing ranks at a complaint from any of the wives, evading their own derelictions with jokes about the woman's *being on the*— what they called the little monthly cloths. It exasperated all the sisters-in-law, who rolled their eyes or pressed their lips together, but at most exchanged glances: to speak of it might've looked disloyal to their husbands.

27

The wind had passed on through and the pines were still when McCoys' driveway ended abruptly in the unfenced clearing. A tangle of downed limbs loomed suddenly in the lights of Les's truck. Around it rose dark shapes of sheds and vehicles, the small locomotive of an old-time tractor, the collapsing fan of an old corncrib. Only two rooms of the sprawling house, one at each end, gave out a dim light. *Naw, he's holed up in his room,* Charlie said on the telephone, and something Les could not understand for the rushing on the wire. After considering all possibilities—including the one he did not believe, that Charlie had behaved with deliberate impropriety—Les had determined to reaffirm mutual respect with the boy just in case the fence line between them had got shoved up a little crooked somehow. It was tricky business dealing with a man people had felt sorry for all his life who'd just been disinherited for no reason. Les's own father, for all his stubborn tyranny, had never shamed one of his sons in public and had dealt generously, if not equally, with all of them. Charlie might need to be reminded—shown—how men ought to act towards each other and each other's families.

Les climbed down from the truck amid a smell of pigs and stumbled in the moonlight among empty barbed-wire reels, a pile of rusty, corrugated iron, old milk cans and washtubs, and, as his eyes adjusted, a white enamel basin that shone like another moon. A dog barked once, and in the shadows of the front porch, Charlie spoke to it and stood up. Nearby, a hog groaned in its sleep.

Charlie had watched Les Gant arrive, waiting between pleasure and fear as long as he dared. Now he descended the ripple-boarded steps, saying softly, "Don't want to stir up the old man."

He led along the porch to the corner of the house, where the canes of a leafless rosebush cast a shadow out into the yard, towards two nail kegs that faced the oil drum where Ian burnt trash. Charlie had chosen these seats as signaling a negotiation rather than a neighborly visit.

The two men sat, and Les spoke of field peas and livestock in the country way that was not really about those things, establishing a familiar rhythm of politeness that seemed to constrain the conversation, and Charlie hated him for that.

Charlie hated him, too, for saying finally, after a pause, "Now I understand there's two sides to every story," and for the careful, respectful speech that followed, where every word reminded you that he was Les Gant.

"Jesus God, I was just laying there to dry off," Charlie said, which was not what he had meant to say at all. "I went to sleep and woke up having to take a piss."

A heavy body thudded against the outside of the house as a hog re-settled itself in a hole against the foundation. "Figured it for something like that. But Charlie——."

Charlie held up his hand—"My apologies for. . .shocking your wife"— and hated that in forgetting the words he had lost the tone: *for the arrival of your wife at the wrong moment?*

Les reckoned she'd get over it. "But Charlie, there's the decencies to think of. I got sisters-in-law all over the place and little nieces coming up, and no telling what females down at Kunkles' liable to take a notion, go up to fish camp. We'd all appreciate it if you'd keep your britches on when you're there."

In that last chance to say he would go nekkid anywhere he wanted on McCoy land and Les Gant couldn't stop him, Charlie managed to reserve, "Skivvies, anyhow," for himself. And he didn't stand up when, after more strenuous politeness, Les did.

"Certain things, old son," he said, "just got to be." And you could think he was the one apologizing, but what Les Gant meant was, *Or else.*

Charlie sat on his nail keg listening to Les stumble his way back to the truck and wondering vaguely at the control the man had over what he said and how he said it. Who did you have to be to get that? Then the truck bumped away through the pines, and Charlie felt mysteriously and unfairly deprived of the opportunity he had seen in this encounter.

28

In the pink daylight of Labor Day, a holiday scarcely noted in union-hostile Texas, Evelyn fried sausage, then eggs in the grease, then slices of light-bread to sop it up, and set three places at the table. Les and Marvin were trucking a young bull to the auction ring; a few cattle were selling by this time.

"Andy McCoy wants to send old Charlie along with a steer," Les had said, with nothing but the *old* to suggest all they'd gone through about him.

"He still thinks Charlie can be sent to do something?"

"Hopes he won't come back, way Charlie's talking, and will I please try to keep him from taking more than half the money from the sale, if there is one." Evelyn wondered if whatever talking-to Les gave Charlie had somehow nudged him towards leaving. She could hope.

When Marvin came in for breakfast, he set two old whisky bottles on the drainboard, full of white corn liquor he bought from a man up in the hills, and she saw that the three men would make a party of it, like old friends. A send-off for Charlie? Who might be in no condition to go after that.

Les could not say whether he would be back in time for dinner. So she was to cook something he might not be able to eat if he was, but never mind. He deserved any day off he wanted to take, and when she finished her chores she would have time to herself, too, could maybe go over to Kunkles', where Al would be out working an ordinary day—but so would Sammy. She did not know what she wanted to do.

When Les and Marvin were gone and she went out into the gentle light and the *oo- OOH* of the doves, she felt the spaciousness of the morning. She and the old cow dog Abe drove the first of the two brown milk cows into the milking shed, where cats gathered and waited, and—she could not do as Papi had been able to, squirt milk from the udder into a cat's mouth—she tipped a sudden little from the first bucket to splash into the pan on the floor. Leaning against the cow's warm, odiferous flank, she could hope she and Les had come through a hard place in their marriage; he hadn't asked her to go to fish camp since he had gone over to McCoys' to talk to Charlie. He might've decided a few fish weren't worth a running quarrel with his wife. She thought of the morning at fish camp when the sun had turned the water to mirror and the place had been given back to her. She could go there today if she wanted to.

She coaxed the cow out of the stall—cows did not like to walk back-wards—and turned her in with her bawling calf. Businesslike, the dog Abe nipped at the second cow's heels without being told. When Evelyn was fin-ished, she half-dragged the heavy milk can up to the house, strained the new milk, and carried the smaller, co-op can out to the road in time for the pick up. Then she washed and scalded utensils and hung them to dry from hooks and branches in the back yard.

At Marvin's house, June filled a green wine bottle with the new milk and put a nipple on it, so Buster and Dilly could feed the big orphan lamb they had made a pet of when it was tiny. Its name, like that of all orphan lambs, was *Waise,* and it grazed now but still came every morning with straw stuck in its greasy wool and bleated at the slat fence where they hung the bottle. Since June was big with another baby, Evelyn went out to the fence with the children to see how fast the half-grown lamb slobbered down the milk. She invited them to come swimming, but they were headed to town to buy shoes. "I'm going to school!" Buster said.

When she got back to the house what she most wanted to do was sit for a while and—what luxury, in the daytime—read, and she took down an old book from the mantelpiece in the bedroom. It was a novel by Charles Dickens that had come to her after Papi died, and she began it and read for more than two hours. It was all different characters, some strange, that did not fit together into a story, but she had read another novel by Charles Dickens and remembered that, by the end, it would. Then it was time to start dinner, and when Evelyn had turned the peas down to simmer, she thought that she would, after all, go down to fish camp because she could, because it belonged as much to her as to Charlie McCoy, and she dug her old bathing suit out of the dresser and went out swinging it by the straps.

At the sound of the screen door slamming, Abe, who hardly knew how to stay at home if anybody was going anywhere, dutifully got up from the shade to trot behind her. The younger dog put his muzzle down and closed his eyes. Evelyn breathed the scent of pines on the trail and felt like herself again.

Under Charlie's tree on the bank, his tackle box yawned open, *Like father like son,* but Evelyn could not tell at the distance whether raccoons had plundered it. Abe chose his spot a short way from the shack, circled in the pine duff, and lay down in the middle of Fish Camp Road. The shack smelled faintly, as always, like fish. In the ritual way of women changing into bathing suits in semi-public places, Evelyn took off her step-ins and pulled the suit up under her skirt; unbuttoned her blouse, unfastened her brassiere, and pulled her arms out of both without taking them off, so as to slip her arms through the straps of her suit and pull it up under those items of clothing before removing them. She folded everything and laid it on the rough wooden table.

Twigs and the scales of old cones were sharp under her bare feet, and she was glad to climb down the bare clay bank and plash into the shallows. Up-river, a speckled young heron rose and flapped slowly away. When she looked downstream, a human floated startlingly in the near distance—who else, she thought, before she even knew it was Charlie.

Charlie raised his head to jeer, "Mrs. Les Gant," and the pleasure sank out of her morning. His presence was like a stain you could bleach and bleach that would always come up again, wet or dry or under the iron.

Evelyn greeted him with a hand before looking back upstream and, aware of her exposed flesh, stepped off into the deeper water and swam away. Then she was sorry, wished she'd said, *The water's too cold,* or anything, and gone right back up the climb-out.

If there had been a place upstream, she could have walked back to the shack, however painfully, through the woods, but in the high bank on that side there was no place—and he would see what she was doing and know she was afraid of him. If she had been downstream of him, there were places she would've tried, or she could've swum and drifted to Gants', or even to Kunkles', though it would fetch comment, showing up in a bathing suit, having to bor-row a pair of shoes to walk home in. And to do any of that, she would have to encounter him, she was sure, in the water.

She determined to ignore him and stay upstream. She stroked smoothly, rolling her head to breathe. When she had made enough distance, she glided, opening her eyes under the water, at a place where it was so clear she could see the rocks on the bottom and, in the sunlight, a small fish glinting away. A school of minnows brushed her legs. She stroked and breathed again, glided again, and was over a deep place as something sizable disappeared into murk below. She was already getting tired. A hovering knot of tiny insects stuck to her face for a moment before the river washed them off. The only practical course seemed to be to drift back down towards the climb-out and go on ignor-ing Charlie. Unless he came there, it would be no worse than when she had climbed in, except she would know he was watching. She floated on her back, seeing a bleached angle of driftwood stuck in a tree, allowing the braiding cur-rent to carry her. She had at least refused to let Charlie deprive her of a swim.

When she turned back over to paddle towards the shelf, she saw he was doing the same, but he had farther to go than she did. He would see her rear end in the skimpy suit, when she climbed the bank, would see the backs of her thighs. *Let him,* she thought, it was only a human body, and how silly this all was. As she stood up in the shallows, he splashed to the shelf.

"What's the matter," he said. "You ain't speaking to me?" As she began to climb, she could see down through the water, he had on pale underdrawers.

"I thought you were going to the auction."

"Naw. Andy went. I 'as thinking I might get a ride that far, but I'ma jump me a train."

Glory hallelujah, if true. "Well, I wish you luck."

"There's mud on your leg," he said, and caught her ankle.

"Charlie!" She tried to kick out of his grasp, but he pretended to be wiping mud off her shin with his other hand. "Stop it. Let me go."

He let go of her ankle, lunged up the bank, and caught her waist with both hands. "Take your hands off me." She leaned half onto the ground at the top; he was pulling her backwards; she caught hold of a tree root.

"I'm just helping you up." He pulled up behind, pressed cold wet underdrawers against her.

"Charlie, this is an outrage."

"Yeah," he said humorously. "It's a outrage, and I don't care, 'cause I'm leaving." He seemed to be teasing but she kicked back hard, hit bone with her heel, and scrambled up as he let go of her. As she reached the shack, the old dog Abe raised his head in the dappled shade and laid it down again.

Inside, she hooked the door, grabbed brassiere and blouse, and pulled arms out of her suit. She stuck them into the other two pieces of clothing before pulling the suit down to her waist but did not stop to fasten more than a button of her blouse.

From behind her he called, "Aw, I'm sorry, I was just funning with you." He ambled up to the door, rattled it against the hook, and peered in through the screen.

She said, "Go away, Charlie. I'm serious," and he said, "All right, all right," and left, but she did not trust him.

She pulled on her skirt, fastened it around her waist, pulled off her bathing suit underneath it, and reached for her step-ins. Then he was back outside in that same leisurely way, so she was expecting some smart remark when a small blade gleamed between door and frame, and she knew, horribly, what he was doing. Did he mean to attack her? To ravish her at knife-point? She looked around for something to fight him with: the benches were attached to the table. He could have no hope of getting away with it except to cut her throat. The faint ordinary roar of a vehicle approaching along Kunkle Road made all that seem impossible.

The door was flung back and he had burst in and seized her before, spring-less on its long slow arc, it had slammed, flipping out the bulging rusty screens of the shack all at once. In the heat it smelled strongly like rotten fish. Then his wet underdrawers pressed against the back of her crumpled-up skirt, with that hard foolish thing in them that was in no wise worth the importance men attached to it, and the knife was on the table, where he had flung it and if she tried to get it and failed, what then?

"Just let me put it in you," he whined, "just once before I go," and pumped against her.

She tried to say, *You've lost your mind,* and couldn't speak.

"Just once, and then I'll be gone for good. You don't know what it means to me."

But she did know, quite clearly: that few seconds of a thing in a hole that male animals lived for and women were stuck trying to regulate. Because of babies. Because people believed a woman's honor resided at the entrance of that hole. Because—there was another reason, but in the growing roar all civilization seemed to have broken down and she could not think what it was. *Let him,* she thought, *just let him.*

"If you must," she croaked.

29

In the rattling, empty cattle truck, Les and Marvin Gant had dropped Andy McCoy at the entrance to his driveway, decided if that was the way he was going to be, they'd finish the last bottle without him, and taken another pull from it. Then, in the time-skipping way of being drunk, Les had nearly hit the corner fence post with Marvin ranting, *You missed, dammit!* as the truck, raked by low-hanging branches—"*Whoa, where'd that'n come from?*"—crunched pinecones down the green tunnel of Fish Camp Road and, bouncing off one side and the other, stripped saplings, alarmed the noon woods, and barked tree trunk big enough to resist into sudden bright wounds.

As the old dog struggled to his feet, adding his deep, announcing *roo-roo-roo*, Charlie, who had not gotten quite into Evelyn, ran out of the shack and, in the long arcing moment before the door slammed, ran back in to fumble up the knife, as if it instead of his overalls or the river was what he most needed; and even before the appearance of the truck, Evelyn, with semen running down her thighs, knew she was forever disgraced. Then the red cattle truck loomed into the clearing and, recognizing it, she remembered Les, who was the other reason she should not have let Charlie do it, and knew as clearly as if she saw the unimaginable future, that the life she had lived was over.

If Evelyn at this moment had been less or more innocent, if she had been her clear-headed self, she might have saved a scrap of that life, might have run out of the fish-smelling shack screaming, *He forced me.* Instead she just stood there, step-ins in her hand, paralyzed by what she had allowed him to do.

Arriving to the sight of a man in his skivvies running away and somebody—the whole situation said *woman*—unidentifiable through the screen of the fish shack, Les and Marvin had so clearly arrived at a scene of wrongdoing that they tumbled out, "Get 'im!" without knowing why they ought to.

Marvin in his rush came first to the angle that allowed him to glimpse through the screen wire and, making out Evelyn, he stumbled and stopped for an instant. Then everything fell together for him with the thought, *She always did think she was too good for us,* and he ran on.

Les's sight of her stopped him cold, almost sober, "Evvie?" She was standing with a small white item in her hands and, when she began to cry and covered her mouth with it, he recognized it as her underwear. "What. . . happened?"

Her inability to reply seemed to say it all. He had suspected for some time that she did not love him in the marital way, and now he realized that the man he had glimpsed running away was Charlie. *So that was it.* A summer's to-do about another man, and that man's decision to leave after Les's confrontation of him seemed to say it all, though there were details Les could not work out just then. Through the rusty screenwire, he saw only an adulterous wife as the explanation and, unable to respond except with his body, ran on.

"It was the knife," Evelyn got out, but Les was gone.

Through the pines, Marvin caught sight of Charlie McCoy clutching jeans, dodging upstream along the bank, suspected what he was doing, and leaped down the bank towards liquid light. In gravel shallows he paralleled his quarry until he caught up with him right before the water would get deep. Sun glinted off the blade of a small open knife in Charlie's hand, as Charlie angled for a dive from the high bank.

"Catch him, hold him." Les had followed through the trees, and Charlie, knife outstretched, dove for the water ahead of Marvin, who tackled a flying leg. The knife flashed out into the water.

In the shallows on the edge of the drop-off, stringy, desperate Charlie and big heavy Marvin splashed briefly until Marvin rolled over on him and sat up. "Let him up," Les gasped from the bank, "you're going to drown him," and Marvin did, a little.

Charlie, spewing and coughing, fought his way to breath and got his elbows under him. Les could see the knife through the water, glimmering on the edge of the limestone shelf. He dangle-jumped down, landed solidly, and waded to get it.

"The little son-of-a-bitch was going to cut me with that," Marvin said.

On the far margin of the pines behind Les lay the wintry stubble-field of his marriage, and he was in a new place. Sober—if a man who had just caught his wife with a half-naked man could have been in any wise sober—Les would have made a careful decision about what to do; drunk, he thought how lucky to have here in his hand the means to cut the little bastard's throat.

But Les Gant, even drunk, was still Les Gant, and the jackknife in his hand seemed like an indecent tool with which to kill a man: a knife like that tightened screws, castrated calves, cut away snarled line, carved burrs out of dogs' coats. If Les had needed a weapon and lacked any other, he would've done what he could with a jackknife, but the knife-fighting moment, if there had been one, had passed. Coldly cutting the throat of a man being held down was a back-alley thing to do.

Suggesting had always been Marvin's role—"If I caught the son-of-a-bitch messing with my wife, I'd cut the nuts off him"—evaluating and choosing Les's. Not only did castrating Charlie McCoy seemed like exactly the kind of hurt Les wanted to inflict on him at that moment, the tool in his hand seemed exactly right for the task.

He seized one of Charlie's suddenly rolling, squirming, kicking legs and knelt across it—*They held my legs,* says transcript of testimony in a trial for the entirely non-fictional crime of castrating a man—and Marvin, still straddling Charlie's middle, seized the other thigh and pulled it up towards him. Medical testimony will detail the wounds.

30

Evelyn, moving against resistance, finished dressing and, feet one at a time on the bench, tied her brown shoes. The air had almost solidified. From upstream, a man's voice began to curse and shriek with a sound like ripping fabric, and she wondered whose that might be. She opened the screen door with difficulty and went out into the clearing. After standing for a minute, she half-crossed it in the thick air towards the woods trail, but, at a change in the tone of the sounds, went on to the bank and looked upstream to glimpse a man who seemed to be Charlie McCoy, flinging up water in the sun as he swam away. *So they didn't kill anybody,* she thought with relief—though she had forgotten who they were and why they might have done so.

Then she could move no farther and stood there without intention or expectation. From across the clearing, Les Gant, who had been her husband, appeared along the bank through the trees with Marvin behind him. Les strode into the clearing as if he did not see her, folding a knife—*the knife!*—with bloody hands, and there was something about it she ought to've said but could not. He looked at her as if she was not there and veered around towards the truck, and she understood that when she had ceased to be his wife she ceased to exist.

"Come on, Abe," he said to the dog, who trailed after him, and there was the sound of the truck door opening, and, after a moment, an arthritic scrabbling as Abe climbed up into the cab.

She went back to where the woods trail opened and escaped along it, but the smell of rotten fish continued, as if her nose had learned it and could not unlearn it, also the geared-down whine of the truck as it burst into view, the dark gleam of the knife under the hook, and the wet fabric pressed hideously against her. She panted in the hot air; her step-ins bunched damply between her legs; her thighs chafed with an alien stickiness. At a white gleam that was the halfway rock alongside the rusty duff, she stopped and remembered that the place she was going did not exist anymore. This seemed to be because she had left the peas simmering on the stove: they had boiled dry, the pot must've caught the wall on fire, and the house had burnt to a shell. In the still, enclosed space of the woods, a general air of ruin lay over everything.

She dawdled along the spongy trail amid the overlapping wavelike swell and subsidence of insect vibration. Where shafts of sun penetrated from distant treetops and seemed to hang without beginning or end, she saw pine bark as if for the first time, its big reddish brown scales oddly alive, outlined in black resin. A man long ago—she could not think who it had been—had measured a tree trunk with his hands: *Ten inches, that is a thirty-year-old tree.* She had never been thirty years old, realized she would never be, now. A single filament of spiderweb that stretched across the trail turned her aside, and she cut through the woods towards the river.

She searched along the high bank for a place better than others, sat down and slid- jumped, not caring for her clothes or the scratches up the backs of her legs. On the gravel, she stepped on the back of one shoe, then the other, and tossed them up onto the bank. She pulled off step-ins as if automatically, pulled up skirt, squatted to wash, rinsed step-ins. She could not climb back up the bank, she thought, then did by way of a small rock and some tree roots and hung her step-ins on a low limb to dry. Exhausted, she sat down on the bank and leaned against a tree. Time stopped.

Later, when it had started up again, it had skipped forward to a yellow and green afternoon of sun above trees, water under pine branches. The river curled over a snag that she seemed to remember had washed down in the big flood, and she listened to the sound it made until she might have slept again. Time had skipped again, and the yellow light was like cane syrup. When it struck nearly horizontal through the trees, a green kingfisher swooped and dropped and plashed and returned repeatedly with a chatter of annoyance to a low limb across the river. Calves bawled downstream, the cowbells on a yard gate shimmered—Evelyn could not remember whose—and, after a long pause, again. The sounds seemed to move her body, and she got up.

She cut into the woods towards the trail and, at the faint p'TRAK, p'TRAK of guinea hens, knew whose they were but could not remember. She took the fork away from them. She came to a familiar rock house she thought had burned sometime before, and there did not seem to be anything to do except open the gate, but when she did, a cow-bell clattered and unfriendly sounding men looked out windows and said things to each other. Gants, she remembered and, from somewhere else, Marvin's face of surprise and something Les Gant ought to have known and did not, back when they had still been married. *He had a knife,* that was it, she could not remember who. Though it was nothing now, she weighed whether to go on in and say it, just for the sake of tidiness.

A man who was Chet Gant called through the screen door, "You got no business here, get on off." The screen was freshly torn at the bottom, as if a dog had dived through it, as she had always tried to keep them from doing. Evelyn hesitated in the yard, tried to speak the one word, *Les,* and could not.

The screen door opened and another man, who was Art Gant, stood in the doorway. "Yeah, go on up to McCoys'." She wondered what he had meant by that.

The cowbell clattered again as she went back out the gate, and Art watched as she turned away up the road, raised her arm for a moment against a streak of light, and went on. He turned back into Les's house and said coarsely to Chet, "McCoy won't do her any good now." Chet forced a laugh.

Les, sick and drunk on the daybed in the kitchen, half sat up; he had heard the clatter of the cowbell. In intervals of waking, he had been waiting for Evelyn. "Who's here?" He knew he had acted without due consideration and, although he could not see how things could be other than they had appeared, he wanted to look into them more carefully. "Evvie?"

"Just a stray," Chet said, and Les lay back down again.

Marvin, on the davenport in the room the young people called the living room, said as he had said repeatedly this afternoon that he never liked her anyhow. The Gant men were waiting for the sheriff, who had called Lester politely to say he was on his way. Gant wives and children were to stay at home behind locked doors and admit *No one but me, not even family, do you understand?*

At another familiar trail that branched off from Gant Road, Evelyn cut through the pines and, through the early accumulation of a red-brown twilight, walked along automatically as if she had known where she was going. She recognized places without knowing why. She came to a newish stile in a wire fence, remembering heartbreakingly that there was something to remember about it, and dawdled there for a while before sidling through. There was the old frame house, *a houseful of people,* where she had once been somebody she was also not anymore.

A surprisingly normal smell of cooking floated out, and a child's wooden wagon in need of paint—she had seen it before—sat in the yard. She had put a hand uncertainly on the wooden gate when a bald man whom she recognized as a Kunkle came out onto the porch and put his fists on his hips.

"You've got a lot of brass to come here, who do you think you are?" he said, and she stood at the gate as if with her body shot away, a head and arms and legs and nothing to hold them together. She knew she was nobody. "Get on back to your rich husband, we don't know you here."

31

She crossed road and fence, spreading strands of barbwire to slip through; what matter if they tore at her clothes, scratched her skin. These things seemed to exist only as adjuncts to the act of walking. Twilight went on rising from the low places. She stopped in a pasture by a brimming water tank and bent to look at a dove so newly dead the ants had not yet found it. She stood up and, without knowing she would do so, touched her mouth to the surface of the tank water and sucked at it. She went on in the gathering dark. Blisters grew and shredded on her feet, the pain a sensation apart from her. She stumbled across fallow fields, past sharecropper houses that stood empty with door ajar; past one with the roof falling in and hollyhocks blooming in a gone-wild garden; past houses where the door was closed and kerosene lamps glowed out onto whitewashed outbuildings. When dogs barked, she bent her path away. She did not know where she was. The moon rose and, as it arced across the sky, more houses lay dark, until all did. She set a foot wrong and, falling, sank into a furrow like water, unable to gather herself again, but after a while her body got up for her and, knowing nothing else, went on. When it could not anymore, it took her all the way up to a dark house because no dogs barked there, and it tried to climb a porch, so that when she fell, she lay there on the hard, swept ground below it.

32

The two old people heard the noise in their sleep in the narrow house that was intentionally no better than a sharecropper's, although the man had inherited it from his father, who had built it on acreage inherited from his father. They had also inherited the wisdom that had allowed all three of them to keep that acreage: *It does not serve a colored man to live in a good house*.

Awakened, the Reverend Mr. Brown asked, "Was that . . .?"

"Yes," his wife said. "Something brushed by the house." It had happened before, a hog, a cow, but there were also many hobos around. Sister and Brother Brown lay listening.

As he moved to get up, his wife said, "Don't," and he didn't. They kept no dogs, lest they drive away some church member in need.

"A loose animal," Sister Brown said, and they lay there for a while and, hearing no more, went back to sleep.

Sister and Brother Brown, like the Sister and Brother White who appear at the beginning of this story, are plot-angels, less important for their individuality than for moving the main character from one life to the next. But this is not to say their individuality is unimportant: on the contrary, it conditions the new lives she may enter. Brother Brown was a small, compact man with a rotund preaching voice, and he and his wife did not get up because he obeyed only God and his wife, in that order. Sister Brown was a long, thin, judicious woman who knew they were shielded by the strong arm of the Lord but might look to a desperate stranger like two helpless old Negroes out there in the country alone.

When the rooster crowed, Brother Brown dressed and went out to look for any sign of what they had heard. He found the young white woman, who wore a gold wedding ring, still asleep on the sweep-patterned dirt below the porch. He went back in to inform his wife.

33

These brown elderly faces bending over her, the old woman touching her shoulder saying gently, "Ma'am?" The difficulty of speaking or moving. The jelly glass of water held to her lips by the old woman who, crouching stiffly, lifted her head up. The tear she could feel running down one temple and into her ear.

"In heaven," the old man says in a resonant voice, "God will wipe away every tear."

When she can move, the strong old woman hauls her up and walks her through a narrow house of bare boards inside, the front room with bed and high old dresser backed by slanting mirror, the back room with ancient wood-fired cooking stove. Unable to remember her name when asked, she sits at a chipped and much-repainted white table, while the woman builds a fire in the stove. Presently the woman kneels to unlace the shoes that stick to her heels with dried blood, to wash the scratches on her legs and her feet, to bandage her feet with torn strips of cloth. She tries to say *thank you* and cannot, cannot even speak when asked if she wants to go outside.

From the steady dry wind, from the prickly leaves of okra and the smooth leaves of peppers, she knows she is still on earth in the late summer. The woman leads her to a cleanly whitewashed outhouse where the light through the cracks comforts her, also the sound of chickens being let out in the morning.

At the kitchen table again, the smell of coffee is valuable. The old man stands over her, placing his hand on her head to pray, "Lord Jesus Christ, whose blood washeth away all sin," so that she remembers she has committed a grave sin, but not what it was.

Grits and egg on a plate. The coffee she can drink, to the woman's voice rising in the next room, "She is not in her right mind." She cannot hear the rest of the words, but her presence seems to trouble these people, and she is sorry. She would say so if she could.

Out again, on the other side of the house, she climbs as directed into the back of an ancient Ford, while the old woman, who is spoken of by the man as Sister Brown, sits in the front and he, spoken of by her as Brother Brown, cranks the engine before climbing in to drive. They travel a long dirt track, then a two-lane dirt road through countryside where tan-and-green pastures lie empty and Evelyn remembers the Depression: the prices of cotton and everything else as far down as anybody has seen them.

When they drive into a town that seems marvelously unchanged, as if it has stood through some disaster that has engulfed everything around it, she remembers its name, Iron Rock. She recognizes the First Baptist Church, as Brother Brown stops in front of it and parks the car. She recognizes, when he has climbed out and accosts a woman on the sidewalk, that he and the woman and Sister Brown are all Negroes and knows then that she herself is white. She begins to understand why she is a trouble, perhaps even a danger, to them.

Which, when he has climbed with elderly difficulty back into the car and driven down the block and turned, and turned again, also makes sense of being left sitting in the car with Sister Brown while Brother Brown walks carefully across dried, late-summer grass and disappears around the side of a big old house. In time he returns, but only Sister Brown must help her out of the car, must hold her arm to lead her across the dry yard and in through a back door. In a bright, high-ceilinged kitchen, a waiting white man in a suit jacket says, "Yes, it's Evelyn Gant"—and that is almost her name, though there is something wrong about it. "Mrs. Gant, I am Brother White." Still she cannot speak.

"I believe she has had a bad shock," Brother Brown says. Then he and Sister Brown leave, joining other people Evelyn cannot yet remember from what she has not yet learned to think of as her old life.

34

She goes where she is led, slumps where set, remembers and understands odd bits about herself and the world. Undressed of her filthy clothes and put to bed by Sister White in a wide nightgown, Evelyn lies in a small room of caramel-colored woodwork at the top of the stairs. She hears Brother White—"of First Baptist," in the hallway below as he introduces himself on the telephone—speaking loudly to people who must live out in the country. He explains to each of them in turn, "A Negro pastor from out at Prairie Hill."

"Yes," he says, "she walked."

Then Evelyn understands that he is speaking about her and, gradually, as the sun heats the attic room, that he is speaking to and about members of her family. In the recurrence of a name, she remembers that she was a Kunkle who married a Gant, and, in other names, such odd bits: Gus in his dark woolen army uniform; Fred saving crickets in a coffee can; her first sight of the human bud that was Liesel wrapped in a blanket; Al, turning his head to speak without moving his body while tying his tie, *before he grew up,* she thinks with mysterious pain. Presently, she can list her siblings in order: August, Frederick, Kurt, Albert—herself in the middle—then Liesel, Greta, Beatrice, and Sammy, him also with incomprehensible pain. Perhaps those who pain her are, like Papi and Mami, dead? *Papi was a rasp, Mami was cream.*

"Then where," the pulpit voice of Brother White rises through the stairwell, "is she to go?" She cannot go to any them, Evelyn understands, because she has committed a grave sin.

Propped up on pillows, she sleeps a little, waking now and then to shadows that have moved across the unfamiliar slant of the ceiling, the unfamiliar sounds of the house below, the voice of Brother White—or did she dream this?—saying, "The sisters I do not fault. They are young, with young families." The smells of cooking that drift up through the house are not Evelyn's, and she has the strange sensation of dwelling on the edge of other people's lives.

Sister White, pale-faced in a starched white apron, climbs the stairs with a tray, a plateful of dinner and a glass of tea with the precious ice in it. "My goodness, it's stifling in here."

She sets the tray across Evelyn's lap, opens the window, and, before leaving, stands a moment in the welcome draft of air from window to door to say earnestly, "Jesus forgives all sins."

How often, and always with a small shock, has Evelyn heard people talk of Jesus this way, as if he was a man down the road, notorious for his regular habits. She eats dinner gratefully. She sleeps again and after she eats supper in the same bed under electric lights, Brother and Sister White stand by the bed together and pray for her out loud.

In the morning Sister White brings Evelyn her own clothes, which have been washed and—who has done such a thing for her?—mended and ironed. "You must dress yourself and come down to the kitchen."

Downstairs, a bowl of oatmeal and a cup of coffee are set on the table in front of her, and Sister White pours milk into the bowl, and Brother White comes in and asks the blessing. Afterwards he says, "Now, you eat this good breakfast Sister White cooked for you, and when you're finished, you get up and help her. She can't run up and down stairs all day feeding you."

Evelyn tries to protest that she does not expect to be waited on, but she cannot find the words for this thought.

"Bring your dishes when you're finished and wash them," Sister White says, and Evelyn, standing at a sink, washes her own and, without thinking about it, the other dirty dishes there.

Sister White is so pleased that Evelyn understands they did not know whether she would do anything for herself or others. To show her willingness, she works in the kitchen all morning, doing such tasks as Sister White gives her, and recovers in the labor something fundamental of herself. After dinner, she sits down to rest and falls asleep in a chair with her head on the table and is put to bed again for the rest of the day.

35

Perhaps it is the next day, or the one after, when Sister White is showing her the back porch where a washboard sits in a deep sink, that Evelyn says without thinking, "Do you have bluing?" and realizes in Sister White's pleasure that she has spoken.

She rubs soap into the cuffs of Brother White's white shirts and understands that by her grave sin she has ceased to be the person she was. After another day on which she falls asleep with her head down on the kitchen table and has to be led upstairs to bed by Sister White, she is prescribed a daily afternoon nap.

On Sunday morning Sister White begs, "Come to church. Come to Jesus," and Evelyn goes as if without volition, to First Baptist where she has been before only to weddings and funerals. She remembers, entering the dark wood interior of the church, that she was a Lutheran, the stately annual procession of liturgical seasons and feasts, of Bible readings belonging to each of them.

As she and Sister White pass down the center aisle to the front row, faces turn, women nudge and hiss, more faces turn, their shock and disapproval quickly rearranged into—what? Some faces Evelyn recognizes dimly—later she will recall distant cousins or girls she knew at school—but none appear to recognize her: her sin has placed her beyond decent people, and the isolation is merely odd.

In the pew, Sister White squeezes Evelyn's hand and confides as if it might be some kind of saying, "'Baptists never give up on anybody.'"

The order of service has the impromptu quality Evelyn recalls from non-Lutheran services. The gospel reading and Brother White's sermon are about the woman taken in adultery and, as Evelyn listens, she begins to suspect that this topic is on her account. She remembers that adultery was, in fact, her sin; then she hopes to find out how she came to do such an extraordinary thing, but Brother White does not talk about her directly. He also seems not to know whether the woman in the Bible story wanted to commit adultery: possibly she did it out of fatigue or irritation or because it did not seem to matter as much as it was made out to. Only, that was an error or the woman would not have been dragged before Christ by the mob.

"Let he who is without sin," Brother White intones, "cast the first stone."

He comes down out of the pulpit and urges, "Repent ye sinners and come to Jesus. Come home to the Truth," but Evelyn does not understand what all of that might mean. She cannot repent what she does not remember.

The choir sings, "Approach, My Soul, the Mercy Seat," and a man she once saw lying unconscious on the street in Iron Rock trudges down the long center aisle. People murmur their recognition. He stands right in front of Evelyn and Sister White; he smells bad. "I've been drunk for two weeks," he declares—it's half a boast—"and I'm a miserable backsliding sinner, God help me."

With an air of tired patience Brother White promises, "He will, brother. Pray, " and prays over him, and reads a passage from the Bible in which Peter comes to Jesus and asks him how often he must forgive a brother who offends against him, and Jesus says, not seven times, but seventy times seven.

The expressions on faces are softer when Evelyn and Sister White go out, and a few people, none Evelyn knows, greet her, though it is not for her own sake but for that of their belief.

Later, while frying chicken, she considers adultery, which would be a sin because—she supposes—it would confuse who was the father of which children; she remembers she could not have children with Les Gant. Adultery would also offend against a man's possession of his wife—here she seems to be getting somewhere—and might cause strife among men. The name Charlie McCoy comes improbably to her and she seems to know a story that some-body—was it she herself?—had committed adultery with Charlie McCoy and there was a terrible fight between him and Les Gant. Though this might be only a rumor, it could explain where she is.

That night she dreams of a gleaming knife and of wet underdrawers pressed against her, and she is frightened and tired and irritated and a voice that is supposed to be Charlie McCoy's, although Charlie McCoy is still in Ft. Worth, whines something she can't quite understand, and there is something important she ought to remember. She wakes with her heart scrabbling in her chest like a dog trying to dig into or out of something.

36

Liesel Kunkle Henderson has never done anything as Richard Henderson's wife that she knew would disappoint him, but on this filmy bright September morning, she dawdles getting out of the house with Kurt and Anna. She can walk them to the Lutheran play-school, now that the family must live in Iron Rock, where Richard and his father eke out a living selling groceries. *Hard times and good, people buy groceries,* Mr. Henderson says, as if to excuse what Liesel would not have thought required excuse. *The knack is getting them to pay.* Behind the yellow brick church, in the dark schoolroom the teacher looks at her with shocked compassion, but Liesel, practiced since her marriage at ignoring people's looks, lingers engaging her in talk about children. Everybody knows Evelyn Gant is Liesel's sister. Richard's parents—to his disappointment, to be sure—regard the disgrace as the inevitable consequence of his marrying a Kunkle. They had wanted him to marry a local heiress. As they seem not to understand, although Richard does, in Prince Carl County the Hendersons are only people who made money in dry goods somewhere else and bought land near Iron Rock to set up as ranchers, much good it's done them.

When Richard will have arrived at work no matter what errand he did on the way, Liesel leaves the Sunday school building by the back, exhilarated by the success of her deception. She considers the alley versus the residential street, chooses the street, and walks along it to the Whites', a groove-columned, four-square house bequeathed to First Baptist by a former member of the congregation. Since a white lady in a hat with a quill on it will attract more attention going to the back door, Liesel goes boldly up the broken concrete to the front. She might be taken for a church member, although anybody recognizing her will know why she is there.

The Whites regard their large, shabby house as a place where church members ought to come in at any time without knocking, so Liesel's knock signals a stranger to Sister White, who comes to the door peering through the screen.

"I was Liesel Kunkle," the woman says, "I understand my sister Evelyn is here. May I see her?" and Sister White thinks, *There is mercy among men.*

The big living room at the Whites' is bare of carpet or rug, also of any expression of personal taste. Sparsely furnished with worn chairs and sofas and tables cast off from church members' houses over the years, it might, with its copies of *The Baptist Standard* and *The Upper Room* scattered around, be a public waiting room, except for its shining cleanliness. Evelyn comes in drying her hands on a white butcher's apron whose strings she has pulled around her narrow waist to tie in front, a familiar contrivance that brings tears to Liesel's eyes.

Since her marriage, the sisters have met only at family events or occasionally at the Lutheran church. As if nothing has happened except this too-long separation, the sisters embrace, Liesel indulging her tears, Evelyn resisting her own as a danger, she does not know of what. Liesel blots her face, her white-on-white embroidered handkerchief like a scrap of something Evelyn was once familiar with.

"Tell me you didn't do it," Liesel begs, and Evelyn, who thinks she must have done but cannot remember, says, "I can't."

Like some other women who knew her as Evelyn Kunkle, Liesel says, "I don't believe it. You never even liked Charlie McCoy."

At the name spoken out loud, Evelyn shudders. "I don't. I can't stand him."

"Oh, no. Did he force you?"

Evelyn's mind splinters and flies apart. "Oh, no." If she sits perfectly still, she may still be Evelyn. "Oh, no," she repeats obligingly.

Liesel, ashamed of her relief, cannot quite register something wrong about the way Evelyn said that. For if Liesel were to pursue Evelyn on the point and she were to say he forced her, then she, Liesel, would have to tell somebody, beginning with the husband who has said to her, not at all unkindly, *This has nothing to do with us.* And, beginning with Richard, who would believe Evelyn, in the circumstances?

"How could you?" Liesel says. "How could you?"

When Evelyn cannot gather her thoughts around the question, Liesel must perceive something wrong with her, "Are you all right, darling *Mamichen?*"

In the lost name, the dangerous pull to emotion. "Oh, quite well, thank you. And you and Richard and the children?"

Thus released and reminded, Liesel embraces her sister again—"My poor darling"—and goes away. Liesel is twenty-three and, except with her children, does not expect to understand things that are wrong. She will regret her inadequate response to her sister for forty years.

From the kitchen Sister White, who has deliberately not listened to the conversation, hears her go and waits to see whether Mrs. Gant will return to the kitchen without being fetched. When she does not, Sister White goes into the living room saying, "How dutiful of your sister to come." Mrs. Gant makes no comment on the visit.

It has yielded, apparently, no invitation to come to the sister's. Perhaps it will be extended later by Mr. Richard Henderson, Sister White thinks charitably. But as the days pass and no invitation comes, Sister White, although she has seen more than her share of people's failings and tries not to judge, is newly distressed at the Kunkles'.

Having by this time had sufficient opportunity to observe Mrs. Gant, she tests an intuition while they are folding laundry in the kitchen. "Do you understand why you are here instead of"—she cannot bring herself to mention the estranged husband—"with your own people?"

Evelyn, who suspects a skein of consequences following on her sin, says, "I have lost my life."

She might better have said *my place in life,* because Sister White must now say, "Jesus promises us that if we lose our life for His sake, we will gain eternal life in heaven."

Evelyn, perhaps having heard this sort of thing too often, is remembering another loss, of the *Verein,* where Papi and Uncle William used to go, and she herself was taken once, but it burnt one night, to a broken frame of charred sticks. *Because people thought the Germans in America were disloyal,* August said, and that was why Gus enlisted in the Army.

"But do you understand, Mrs. Gant, what the loss of your old life means for your future here in the world?"

Children are the future, Mami used to say, and Evelyn remembers Sammy at the baptism of Kurt and Ellen's baby, the last year Mami was well enough to go to church. Sammy was seven, wearing short pants, and standing up front at the font to see, and he must've had a mosquito bite behind one knee, because just as the pastor was saying, "Ernst Frederick Kunkle, I baptize thee"— Sammy folded up his leg and, with the toe of his Sunday shoe, scratched behind his knee. How Les Gant, who had not wanted to go, laughed about that afterwards.

"We are all grown now."

That evening, Sister White closes the door of Brother White's study to say to him, "I do not think Mrs. Gant fully understands what has happened."

"Then you must tell her."

How could Sister White say the words for that? But kindness alone requires that she say something before the District Attorney comes. She prays for guidance.

37

A copy of the previous week's *Iron Rock Standard* may be Jesus' answer, folded under the short leg of a Sunday school piano bench, where Sister White discovers it while arranging chairs for the Women's Bible Study and Missionary Union. Recognizing the tattered unfold, she carries it home, where Mrs. Gant—what a wonderful housekeeper! what a novel blessing in Sister White's life!—wields a dust mop in the living room.

"My dear," Sister White says, "I thought you ought to know about the prosecution." Evelyn looks as if to discover she herself is being prosecuted.

Sister White leads her to the sofa. "You will want to sit down to read it." The headline is, "Gant Trial Set."

[September 25] *The trial of Lester Gant, Junior, and Marvin Gant both of Iron Rock has been set for 10 A. M., Tuesday October 6, in District Court in Meusebach. The case will be tried before Judge John M. Meister, with District Attorney Andrew Burrell prosecuting. The Gant brothers, prominent Prince Carl County stock farmers are charged with the castration of a neighbor,*

Charles McCoy, who is reported to be recovering.

The bloody knife in Les's hands, the cursing voice like ripping fabric overwhelm her, and Evelyn leans back against the worn upholstery until she feels the springs in it. Then she seems already to have known, only forgotten. *The Gants are also defendants in a civil action brought by Charles McCoy against them.*

With trepidation over whether she will find her own name, she goes on to another article on the same page. This article will be referred to in legal proceedings as prejudicial: *Everybody in Iron Rock knows Les and Marvin Gant, and the mouth of Iron Rock is still agape at the news. Said a leathery, crinkled man leaning against the Iron Rock post office, "They're fine young men, or at least we used to think so."*

The Gants are the two oldest of the five sons of Lester Gant, Senior, owner of a 4,000-acre ranch west of town. Les Gant, 32, is his father's second in command and a forward-looking farmer. "It was Les talked his father out of cotton," August Kunkle, a neighbor, recalled, "right before the rest of us went broke in it." Les Gant is widely regarded as a sober, upright citizen, not the kind to get involved in any wildness. Evelyn looks at the name of the writer, whom she knows slightly.

People around Iron Rock seem to think Marvin Gant, 29 and sociable, might be a different story. Though known as a hard worker, he could often be found at the barbershop on a Saturday afternoon with a young son, and is remembered from his youth as a fighter.

When single, he used to make every dance for miles around. Once, according to an informant who requested anonymity, Marvin fought a man because he did not like his coat, calling it to his face, "a finicking, highfalutin, white-shoe sort of a coat." When the owner of the coat took exception to these remarks, Marvin whipped him soundly but the next day drove twenty miles to apologize. Evelyn had not heard that story, but it sounds like him.

People call Marvin Gant "open," "generous," "loyal," "a braggart," and "too fast with his fists." Marriage and fatherhood, people thought, had settled him down.

Now the state will try to prove that he and his brother, free on bond meanwhile, did knowingly and willingly, with malice aforethought, castrate a neighbor, Charles McCoy, 25. And it will ask the jury to send them to the penitentiary for 15 years, the maximum penalty for castration.

Clutching the paper as if the touch of it has power, Evelyn reads on into the sort of thing people have always said about the Gants: *By most people's standards rich from birth, the Gant brothers used their talent, effort, and opportunity to build solid positions for themselves in the community. Most people in Iron Rock think they have thrown those away. A patriarch summed it up, "Don't matter how that trial comes out, those boys are hurt real bad."*

Without knowing why, she thinks how much has followed from how little.

38

District Attorney Mr. Burrell, accustomed to driving around the county lining up witnesses who cannot or will not come to the courthouse until compelled, arrives in his tan summer suit at the Baptist preacher's in Iron Rock, sets down his briefcase to free his hands and, as he does habitually, pulls up his trouser legs slightly before sitting. He asks Mrs. Gant the questions he will ask her in the courtroom, though he need not use the words he must use there.

The case is distasteful to him and, in the interest of asking as few questions as possible, he begins with simply, "Where at the fish camp were you when Les and Marvin Gant arrived?"

The man's way of asking questions takes Evelyn off guard, and, at the word *fish camp,* she is there in the hot, rotten-fish smell of the shack, with the whining cattle truck, the nose of its worn red cab crashing into view, until Mr. Burrell says, "Mrs. Gant, you must answer the question," and she does not remember the question.

But later, after he asks her, "Was Charles McCoy inside the shack with you?" the blade of the jackknife gleams between door and frame, and she is grateful to be asked again.

"Yes," she says, even though now he will ask her what she cannot remember.

But he seems to care nothing about her act of adultery, only about its consequences for the men. "What did Charles McCoy do when Les and Marvin Gant arrived?"

Then Charlie is out of the shack, the unsprung screen door swinging back on its long arc before he runs back in and grabs up the knife from the splintery table and runs back out again, and she recognizes the truck and, in the loose slam of the screen door, her life is over.

"Mrs. Gant?" Mr. Burrell says.

"He took the knife and ran."

"So Charles McCoy had the knife when he was in the shack?" Mr. Burrell says in a moment of apparent interest, but it seems to be about something else.

"Did you hear sounds of a fight, from the riverbank, after that?"

She remembers, "They were below the riverbank," and the man's high curses, like ripped fabric, and thinks of course it had to be Charlie, because Tessa would not tolerate any of her boys cursing.

When Mr. Burrell leaves her alone, it is not a bad thing to be, and she sits on until Sister White comes downstairs—"You must be tired"—and walks her upstairs for her nap. Evelyn lies awake all afternoon, safe in the blessed present.

39

She is on the back porch shining his Sunday shoes when Brother White comes out to say, "Mrs. Gant, when you are finished with your labors, let me speak to you in my study." The study door is open except when people go in to speak privately with Brother White, but when Evelyn goes in, he leaves it open. The small room is dusty: she is not allowed to clean in there.

She sits on a lumpy fat chair and he says, "Mrs. Gant, as you know, you may be called to speak at the trial of your husband's brother on charges of assault." He is ponderous, with a sometimes severe manner, and she might have disliked him if she had not understood that he feels responsible for people's souls. "Concerning your own part in that crime, I believe you will feel better if you unburden yourself to me, although you need not."

"I cannot."

"Sister White also stands ready, if you would find it easier. . . .."

"I cannot." A broken spring is poking the back of one of Evelyn's thighs, but she does not want to shift in the chair.

"Mrs. Gant, whether you confess to any human, there is one Person you do need to unburden yourself to, and that is Jesus, who forgives sin and offers new life in Him."

For the first time, the phrase, *new life,* sticks in Evelyn's mind like a grass burr: she seems to have no life, only this skein of consequences to follow out. But where will it go?

On Sunday, Brother White preaches a sermon against "Bible-destroying, evolution-believing, deity-of-Christ-denying German rationalism," and Evelyn, not to look at him, looks at the maroon carpet ubiquitous in big churches and wonders if he thinks that, being German, she is an evolution-believing rationalist. She has heard of evolution, and she would've thought from the name that *rationalist* would be good, but she doesn't know what one is.

40

In the cool, dim, wood-paneled courtroom belonging to Prince Carl County, where murmuring visitors fill the public section, voices from the hallway reverberate into a roar, and the Gants, led by Lester, file in down the defendants' side. Still muscular and heavy, Lester shows no sign of the change that began in him when he took out a mortgage he knows he will be unable to repay. He stands aside as Les and Marvin, followed by the lawyers from Iron Rock and San Antonio, then Chet and Art and—summoned home from the CCC—even Parker, seem to over-fill the room. Lester and the younger three file into a row as close as possible to the defendants' table, as if the important thing is to concentrate their force at the right point.

More than one observer might watch to see them look across the aisle at the woman who is still Les Gant's wife but, to a man, they avoid it. All but Les refuse to be seen by their neighbors to look; Les refuses to be seen by his father and brothers. He has failed them, especially Marvin, whom, instead of joining in with, he ought to have kept from doing anything this bad. The unseemliness of their attack on Charlie repulses Les: he ought to have horsewhipped him— sort of thing they used to do—sued him for a dollar in damages, visited disgrace on him instead of on himself and his own family, who have loyally closed around him. His father, who would've been justified in disowning him and Marvin, has hired the best lawyers in the state to defend them and taken out a mortgage to pay them, which he will answer no questions about. This unreproachful support, everything to Les now, creates its own difficulty: questions about Evelyn that he can make no opportunity to ask her torment him like a swarm of biting flies. He can't doubt her guilt: if she had somehow been innocent, she would've come home instead of wandering around the countryside to be sheltered by strangers. But why did she betray him with Charlie McCoy after a summer of trying to avoid him? Did he himself push her into it? Did she do it hoping to conceive and—as she had seemed willing to do by adopting—to raise another man's child as his? If he used or invented some errand to town to go to the Baptist preacher's house and ask for her, word would get back home almost before he did. He can imagine how Lester would take that.

From the boom of voices in the hallway Old Man McCoy's voice breaks free to complain Biblically, ". . . has deprived me of heirs to send me lonely into old age," and the others fall silent beneath it. Two Gants share a skeptical glance, *As if he doesn't have Andy, as if Charlie had been the old man's heir*, a condition they all expect Charlie's civil suit to change.

Land thief, Lester thinks, and imagines Evelyn carrying Charlie McCoy's child, himself pointing her out to Old Man McCoy, *There's your heir, you father of a woman stealer, the bastard of a thief and a whore.*

Old Man McCoy, with the unkempt gray hair of a prophet, leads his two sons into the courtroom, Charlie uneasy and cocky. He looks at Evelyn openly enough, glad to've dragged her down to his level, glad to've disgraced Les Gant, not that he'd've done it if he'd known what it would cost.

When the proceedings finally begin to crank up, defense attorneys request a change of venue, arguing that widespread discussion of the case, the prominence of families involved, and newspaper stories—one in particular is cited—have been prejudicial to their clients. The motion is denied, but the point will be proved as prospective juryman after juryman is disqualified.

Most of the people in the courtroom, including Evelyn and members of the public who have gotten seats with such satisfaction, can hear little of what is going on in the section where prospective jurors sit to be questioned. Most of them have already formed opinions about the case. One group believes Les and Marvin should never have been charged: a man's finding his wife with a nearly-naked man who ran at the sight of him seems provocation to do worse than Les Gant did; and what could Marvin do but support his brother at such a time? Their act, if a crime at all, was a crime of passion, its proper penalty the damage to reputation that will linger around them for the rest of their lives and their family name for as long as anybody remembers it.

Other men's imaginations are worse afflicted by the act itself. For weedy, unlikely-looking young McCoy to have been fooling around with a fine-looking Gant wife seems like less of a crime than an accomplishment—her husband ought to have kept her at home. A populist strain to this party of opinion casts the McCoys, known from the old man to be contentious and hard up, as underdogs to the numerous and prosperous Gants. Should two men get away with an act like that because of who they are? One prospective juror says loudly that the defendants ought to be hanged, and Marvin laughs but Les looks deadly serious. If the offended husband had killed McCoy, opinion would've had to acquit him; as it is, McCoy seems to have been visited with cruel and unusual punishment.

After three days, state and defense attorneys have qualified only seven jurymen, and Judge Meister ends the questioning by admitting that it would be "almost impossible" to get a fair-minded jury in Prince Carl County.

41

Evelyn, staying within three blocks of downtown Iron Rock, never goes farther than the Whites' yard alone. She has left the glass-paned back door unlatched so she can carry in the basket of laundry stiff from the line, and when she pushes through the door she overhears Brother White: "She cannot stay here forever."

"She is the best of workers," Sister White says. "Surely a place can be found for her."

"The difficulty," Brother White is saying as Evelyn closes the door, but Sister White shushes him, so all Evelyn hears after that is, ". . . a notorious sinner into their homes."

42

At the different county seat where the Gants and their lawyers will stay at the only hotel, it is thought unseemly for Evelyn to stay at the boarding house with the male witnesses. A place is found for her with, say, an elderly Baptist widow on the quiet, tree-grown courthouse square, several blocks from the commercial district. Driven in the car by Brother White to protect her from a possibly unsafe train journey, Evelyn glimpses low steps, the rise of white columns and, through the tops of leafless trees, the greenish copper dome of the courthouse. She is admitted to a shuttered bungalow, where an old woman, according to Sister White the widow of a longtime clerk of court, chats pleasantly with Brother White. She addresses scarcely a word to Evelyn, only a face wrinkled in disapproval as she shows her to a bedroom full of furniture and multiply-draped windows. The woman will bring Evelyn's supper to the room on a tray, and her breakfast, as if she must neither eat with her nor wait on her at table. At time to go across to the courthouse, she grips Evelyn's wrist with two hard fingers like a handcuff.

This courthouse, in its residential setting, looks so different from the one in Meusebach that the sameness of its interior odors is startling to Evelyn: pine tar floorwash and the linger of old cigar smoke, sloshing cuspidors like the chamber pots of old, left unemptied too long. Outside the courtroom Evelyn comes face to face with Lester Gant, who has detached himself from a circle of men to gaze with calculated rudeness from her face to her middle. She lowers her glance, discovers a satisfaction in having known for months what he must wait several more to be sure of, and goes on in.

The Gants, in their ill-fitting, unaccustomed suits, their starched white shirts and refusal of neckties except by Les and Marvin, stick together and move as a body in public. Waiting for their lawyers, they cluster outside the courtroom where, inside, anything may happen. In the civil trial, the judge, after finding the obvious, that Charlie McCoy had been cut by Les and Marvin, also found that he ought to be compensated with twelve thousand of Lester's borrowed dollars.

Standing among them, Les's glimpse of Evelyn, who has skirted them, makes him ashamed of a vision he had of encountering her alone in an empty hallway and asking her, reducing all his questions to one, *What really hap-*

pened, back there? He is ruined no matter what, can hope at best for the cau-terization clarity might provide, such the civil trial had no interest in offering. The lawyers arrive, and the Gants form up and file into the courtroom, where Les hopes for Marvin's sake that they get off, or a light sentence.

A jury is chosen. In the afternoon, opening statements are made. With a few dadoes and finials, the State plans to prove about the same as the McCoys have already proved to the satisfaction of the civil court. The defense proposes to show that the two defendants, with minimal help from Andrew McCoy, drank nearly two fifth-gallon bottles of whiskey on September 7 between 10 A. M. and 1 P. M., when they discovered the wife of one of them in compromis-ing circumstances with Charles McCoy at a fishing camp, where they were so drunk they do not remember what they did. This seemed true when it was first suggested to Les; *true enough for a court of law* was Marvin's expression. The little he had remembered at first seemed unutterably private to Les: his en-counter with Evelyn at the fish shack; his realization—when?—that the man who had run out of the fish shack was Charlie McCoy; the blinding reflection of sun off water as he knew that all the good remaining to him came down to having a pocket knife in his hand; his avoidance of Evelyn when he folded it. What Les remembers now would be hard to say, after all he has heard.

On a second day, the prosecution begins to call its witnesses. Andrew McCoy, concerning the condition, direction, and expressed destination of the defendants when they left him at the entrance to his family's driveway. Then Evelyn—whom Les must appear to look at on the witness stand without actu-ally doing so—concerning the arrival at fish camp of the Gant cattle truck empty of cattle.

"Was Marvin Gant driving the truck?"

She cannot mention Les directly, can only be led to allude to him. "No."

"When the men arrived in the truck, was anyone else at the fishing camp?"

She testifies to the presence of Charles McCoy, whose whereabouts the prosecution seeks to establish—"In a screened shack where Fish Camp Road ends," she says reluctantly—and his actions when the cattle truck arrived.

"He ran out of the shack."

A man in his skivvies, running from the shack, Les remembers clearly. Not yet Charlie.

"Mrs. Gant, in what direction did Charles McCoy run?"

Question by question, she testifies: he ran towards the river; Marvin jumped down from the truck and ran after him—"Was Marvin Gant alone in his pursuit of Charles McCoy?" "No he was not."—the sounds of a fight "on or below" the riverbank; the shouts of men, the screams of one man.

To the next question, Evelyn does not respond at first; it has to be asked twice. She emerged from the shack and walked to the riverbank in response to the screams, to see Charles McCoy swimming upstream, "Towards Mc-Coys'," and, from the way she says it, Les understands that whatever was between them is over.

The defense wishes to cross-examine her, and the courtroom seems gratified. The defense must remind the jury whenever possible that Les—with Marvin as his loyal brother—had cause for what they argue they cannot remember doing, and the courtroom is full of men who have come to hear about that cause.

"Mrs. Gant, why had you gone into the fishing shack?"

She had been swimming, she says. "I was changing out of my bathing suit into my clothes."

When Charlie came in? Les would like to know that, but she is not being, as another lawyer reminded Les and Marvin, sued for divorce here.

"What was Charles McCoy wearing when he ran out of the shack?"

"The underdrawers in which he had been swimming."

"Had you gone to fishing camp that day to meet Charles McCoy?"

"No, he—."

"Was Charles McCoy often at the fishing camp?"

"Yes."

The prosecutor objects that this line of questioning is argumentative, as Les was told would happen. *The point is just to get in as much as we can about it.* Then that's all from Evelyn, and Les is painfully relieved as she is escorted back to the witnesses' section.

The prosecution calls Charles McCoy, this man Les had thought of as one of his own. When he is sworn to tell the truth, Les would like to laugh at the idea; there is Charlie in the moonlight saying, *Jesus God, I was just laying there to dry off.*

"Mrs. Gant has testified that when you saw the defendants, you ran towards the river. Is that true Mr. McCoy?"

"Sure it's true." Charlie swaggers with the confidence that means to cover its lack in certain men.

"Where were you when you next encountered either of the defendants?" Les wonders where he himself had been.

"I was up on the riverbank and I seen Marvin coming along below."

"At this time you had a pocket knife in your hand, is that correct?"

"Sure I did."

"Was it open or closed."

"Open."

"And where was Les Gant at this time?"

"He 'as coming through the woods after me." Then Les remembers with satisfaction running through the trees along the riverbank after a Charlie who was carrying something that hung up for a moment on a tree trunk before he ripped it free.

"What did you do then, Mr. McCoy?"

Les listens for what might start memory. "I dove off the bank and Marvin grabbed at my legs." He himself might not even have seen that, running through the trees.

"What happened to the knife then, Mr. McCoy?"

"Knocked it clean out of my hands."

"Did you see where it went?"

"How could I see where it went when I was trying to keep Marvin Gant from drowning me?" But Charlie must answer in the courtroom way.

"Where was the knife when you saw it again?"

"In Les Gant's hand, when he come up out of the water with it."

"Had he had dived into the water after you?"

Still too shallow, Les thinks, seeming to remember that he had known even in his drunkenness not to dive there, but Charlie says he did.

"What happened then, Mr. McCoy?"

"Marvin was a-sitting on me in the shallow water, and he said Les ought to cut my nuts off, and they held my legs up, and Les he went to cutting on me." And Les remembers the intention but nothing of the doing.

"What did you do, Mr. McCoy?"

"Shoot, I was kicking and yelling, and there was blood running down, and I seen one of my nuts drop into the water. I seen it! And I landed a kick in

Les Gant's face and he let go of my leg, and I got my foot down on the gravel and shoved out from under Marvin."

Les remembers only the bruise and the painful jaw of the days that followed and his gratitude for them. *You'd think a man would remember a kick in the face.*

Re-examined by the prosecution, Andy McCoy testifies that after he arrived home his brother Charles McCoy appeared from the direction of the river, wearing bloody wet underdrawers "with blood running down his leg," and that he, Andy, drove him to Prince Carl County Hospital.

The prosecution calls Dr. Mayfield Beck of Meusebach, who testifies, as at the civil trial, to "a scrotal wound" to Mr. McCoy, "which appeared to be three separate lacerations, one being exactly across the top part of the scrotum from side to side, a second being along the right side of the scrotum in an up and down direction, and a third that branched out from it in more or less the form of an inverted Y."

I've done it in the dark, Les thinks, and of calving, the warm slick body, the wounds to dress with pine tar oil, those ordinary things that seem now lost to him, whatever happens.

Cross-examined by the defense, Dr. Beck cannot swear to the absence of a testicle. "I wasn't counting testicles, I was repairing an injury that had occasioned a good deal of bleeding and swelling." He can swear, as he did at the civil trial, to the presence of one testicle *Probably saved us another twelve grand,* Marvin said. Dr. Beck is pressed to acknowledge the possibility that Mr. McCoy may not have had a second testicle at the time of the attack.

The sheriff of Prince Carl County swears that, when he examined the premises of the fishing camp late on the afternoon of September 7, nothing that might've been Charles McCoy's testicle was found. *Meat for a fish,* men think, and queasily of eating such a fish.

The prosecution rests its case.

43

When she is alone in the stall, where around her feet the outline of many small tiles rises like chicken wire and floats, she leans her head against the wooden door. The nose of the worn red cab bumps into view, and Les stops at the angle in the rusty screen wire where he can see her, *"Evvie?"* and she can do nothing but press her step-ins to her mouth. Then women come in talking, their voices knocking around the hard room, and her body knows what to do, and her hands know, and when she gets up again, they arrange things without her having to think. The floating, entangling layer of chicken wire has receded to a ladies' room floor, and she goes out and stands at the sink, where the dark wooden roller holds a continuous towel. She has never fainted in her life and is not going to start doing so now, in a courthouse full of men who laugh at Charlie in wet underdrawers and take no interest at all in the knifeblade gleaming under the big hook on the door. *Mrs. Gant?* the prosecutor said, as perspiration ran down the sides of her body inside the dress she must wear for as many days as the trial lasts, and her body, hands clutching at the hard slick arms of the witnesses' chair, knew what to do and she did not faint. The women come out of their stalls speaking and she misses Sister White, with her kindness and her carefully untroubling small news of church and neighbors.

44

Les dreads his own shameful defense, which, for its first witness recalls Andrew McCoy. This will be about *the corn, hooch, skee, the cause of it all,* which Les wishes he could believe it was. He never even liked it much, thinks he might never drink again, though, on the other hand, now why not?

"Mr. McCoy, approximately how much liquor had you and the defendants consumed together?"

"Most of a couple of fifths. There was a couple of inches left in one of them."

"Would you estimate that you had shared it equally?"

"Nowhere near that."

"When they parted from you, as you testified earlier, with the intention of going to the fishing camp to finish the bottle, would you say that you were sober?"

"Not strictly, no, but I'd gone at it easy, 'cause I couldn't afford to take the day off." That was what Les had thought too, when Marvin set the bottles on the drain-board—that faraway, impossible-seeming morning.

"So the defendants had drunk most of it?"

"They had."

For its next witness, the defense calls the Superintendent of the State Hospital in Austin, a physician "expert on conditions of the mind," who testifies that the amount of whiskey drunk by the Gant brothers on September 7th could cause the two men to black out but not necessarily go to sleep. The effect could be a temporary insanity in which they would not know right from wrong.

"And they would not afterwards remember what had happened during this period of 'black out'?"

"Yes, sir, that is correct."

Charles McCoy is re-called, the attention of the courtroom is again fixed, and Les prepares himself as if for a burn: *We'd been at it all summer, she was wild for it, we was going to run away together.*

Charlie testifies that he had been fishing and swimming in the river, "like I did most every day," and he was in the fishing shack with Mrs. Gant.

"What were you doing there, Mr. McCoy?"

Charlie sniggers, and the prosecutor objects that the question is argumentative, but the judge instructs the witness to answer.

"Messing with a piece of . . .fishin' gear." Men laugh, the judge pounds his gavel, and Les holds onto the lawyer's words, *It may save you and your brother from going to prison.*

"Why did you run out of the fishing shack at the approach of the truck?"

"'Cause I was in there in my drawers with Les Gant's wife." Men laugh again and the judge gavels them silent.

"Had you been, ah, swimming with her?"

"Sure I had, ain't nothing wrong with that."

"About the pocket knife that you had in your possession when you were in your underwear." Evelyn listens as if for a moment there is some kind of hope. "Where did you get this knife?"

"From my tackle-box."

"Why was that, Mr. McCoy?"

"Reckoned I might need it." Rowdy laughter, and the judge threatens to clear the courtroom.

When? Evelyn thinks, but the prosecutor does not ask that.

"Was the knife open or closed when you last had it in your hand?"

"Reckon it 'as open."

Rather suddenly, Charlie's testimony is over.

Lester Gant, Jr., is called and, being sworn, looks out at the audience in the courtroom. "Tell us, Mr. Gant," the lawyer says kindly, "what happened after you left Andrew McCoy at the entrance to his driveway?"

And Mr. Gant is sorry to say, he does not remember leaving Andrew McCoy at the entrance to his driveway. "You were driving the cattle truck with your brother in it, were you not, Mr. Gant?"

"I reckon I must've been." He had left the auction ring with Andy McCoy and Marvin Gant in the cab with him, "So I reckon I was, and it stands to reason we'd've dropped Andy off at his place on the way back to ours," but Les does not remember any of that.

He does not remember arriving at the fishing camp. He does not remember climbing out of the truck and chasing off after Charles McCoy. If Les were asked whether he remembers seeing his wife in the fishing shack, he would have to say he does, but he is not asked that and will not be, in this trial. He does not remember jumping into the river, or finding the knife, or cutting Charlie McCoy. "I reckon I might've under the circumstances," he says, "but I don't remember doing any of it."

Marvin, who follows Les into the witness box, follows him in all he has said, only remembering nothing after they got into the truck at the auction ring and adding, "May God strike me dead if I knew a thing about any of it." This is a flourish, Les knows, because Marvin also remembers seeing Evelyn at fish camp. But God does not strike him dead.

The jury takes forty minutes to find the Gant brothers guilty as charged.

45

On the following day, a bright cold Friday a few days before Christmas, character witnesses testify that Les Gant is a leader in the community and Marvin Gant is "the best fellow in the world, no harm in him at all." Mr. Albert Kunkle appears—although Evelyn had somehow thought he was dead—

declaring that the Gants have been the best of neighbors, time out of mind. *Who do you think you are?* he says to her from the porch, and she stands with her body shot away.

Les and Marvin are sentenced to the minimum of five years, and defense attorneys announce plans to appeal. A motion to release the Gant brothers on the bond they have already posted is denied, which Evelyn, not knowing quite how those things work, understands to mean they must go to jail immediately. That night, her last in the suffocating silence of the elderly widow's house, she thinks with self-reproach of Les and Marvin in jail.

But the next day, being driven by Brother White through the commercial district on the way out of that town where she will never be again, she glimpses Les on the street from the rear window of the Essex. The sight fills her with emotion, although it seems to be about her life, not simply her past, as she cannot think of herself as having a future.

So she cannot imagine a time in which anybody might want to know about her past—the one I've invented for her because an eleven-year-old character who could not have been born yet will want to know about it; the past that, with just that glimpse of Evelyn's future might've been enough for my story, which might end here, if it had been different. It can't quite: some of its actions, places, motives, allusions, other characters, interactions, and so forth having deliberately or accidentally implied dramas in her future. In a human life that sort of thing could be regarded as incidental—an aura around a person of what we can't know—but a fictive life ought to be less ragged, fiction being different from life in that way as in many others. Which is to say that my story in the telling has accumulated additional purposes.

These now require that Evelyn's future be farther imagined, so that, after the days of solitude and traumatic memory in the distant county seat, she must be returned to the comparative friendliness and protection of the Whites', where circumstances, however, are changed for her.

46

As if Evelyn must now confront the world, she is sent on errands to downtown Iron Rock, to grocery, post office, hardware store, where she is stared at, treated impatiently, leered at by men. The strangeness of these experiences strikes her with what it was to be the person she used to be. One bright cold day she sees the newlywed Beatrice from half a block away down the board sidewalk, and the sight is like a rush of sweetness in the mouth, a pain at the root of the tongue. Beatrice, accompanied by a young woman friend, crosses the street, an act that, given the arrangement of stores and so forth, can be for no reason but to avoid Evelyn. On the boardwalk she seems for a breathless moment to have seen what her life has shrunk to.

Still awed, she comes in by the kitchen door to the house that has begun to feel like home. Here is Sister White in the kitchen, and Evelyn would almost like to say, *I saw my baby sister on the sidewalk and she crossed the street to avoid me.* The sight of a place laid for her as usual at the kitchen table stops her.

As often while Sister White works around the house, she has been praying about her concerns, and she looks at Evelyn with affectionate plea: "I was just praying for you to repent and come to new life." Her prayer has been given urgency by the need to find another place for Mrs. Gant to live: the wife of a Baptist minister cannot be suspected of sheltering an unrepentant sinner merely for household labor.

I don't think Evelyn, as the character I have imagined, can understand this; she can at most feel her hosts' desire that she move out into a world where she has forfeited her old place. A few years later, after her first elderly incontinent patient dies, when a second demented bedridden parent of a church member is found to require her care, she will understand that her earthly life has been in this wise secured for her by the Baptist community. But as to foreseeing any such benefit to the religious conversion that, on this cold day in the warm kitchen, Sister White prays for her to experience, no, I don't think Evelyn is capable of that. So she can't intend to achieve or perform a religious conversion as she carries a bowl of winter vegetables, the rounds of orange and white, the ruched slivers of palest green, from the kitchen into the chilly dining room to set on a crocheted mat.

Rather, she feels intense gratitude to Sister White and the desire to please this sympathetic friend, provider of all care and affection for four post-traumatic months. That is to say, the process of Evelyn's conversion will be psychologically genuine: under Sister White's steady influence, she begins to wonder whether she does, in fact, repent.

Brother White's altar calls are extended at the rate of twice a week, and at the next of them, on Wednesday night, the events of Labor Day as Evelyn knows them blunder through her mind one by one like calves through a chute. That she went to fish camp; that she swam even though Charlie was there; that she was in the shack with the door hooked when he inserted the knife blade under the hook; that after the cattle truck came, when Les saw her, she was standing there with her step-ins in her hand; and that, when his look said he was through with her forever, she said nothing, though she ought to have said, *He had a knife.* She regrets all of those acts, for their consequences.

But repentance, as she was briefly instructed in a Lutheran catechism class some twenty years before, is different from regret: less a response to consequences than to having offended against God's Perfection, which we are wholly to love. Concerning Perfection Evelyn has no difficulty: she sought to be a perfect wife and repents her inexplicable failure; she sought to be a perfect *Mamichen* and repents having abandoned her position only to visit disgrace upon beloved children.

"Repent ye sinners and come to Jesus," Brother White urges.

In the shadowy, sparsely filled church, Evelyn repents what she remembers and what she knows she must have done. She does not answer the altar call.

But her posture may have given away her thoughts: Sister White wears an arch look afterwards and sings in the kitchen, *"The blind man stood on the road and cried, The blind man stood on the road and cried, The blind man stood on the road and cried, . . Oh, my Lo-rd, save me."*

On Sunday the gospel reading is a familiar passage in which Jesus is given to begin, "Let not your heart be troubled," and to end, "I am the Way, the Truth, and the Life." Evelyn thinks her way through the three during the sermon, which is unhelpful to her in doing so. That she needs a Way, she understands. And certainly Jesus said many true seeming things, but what Truth, spoken of in that manner, could mean, she has never understood. The only person who asks in the gospels is their great villain, Pilate, who is scoffing— the point apparently being that one is to believe and not ask questions. But how can she believe what she does not understand? She turns to the matter of Life as far easier: the desire to live gathers itself in her like hunger.

Brother White comes down out of the pulpit to urge any present who know themselves in need, "Come to the mercy seat. Repent and receive the gift of new life." His glance takes in Evelyn.

Sister White urges, "Go on. We'd so love to have you." It's been nearly five months since anyone has said anything like that to Evelyn. The choir sings softly the popular new "Church in the Wildwood," with its *Come, come, come, come.*

To small intakes of breath behind her, she gets up, not knowing what she can truthfully say. *I can't believe as I ought to? I can't remember committing the sin I know I did?* She turns and looks at the fan shape of eyes spread out from the aisle like a butterfly's wings. She says simply, "I committed adultery," and a collective sigh says it's enough.

"There is more joy in heaven," Brother White declares, "over one sinner who repents than over ninety and nine just persons," and she is someone again, the repentant sinner.

"Hallelujah," a man calls, and other congregants look a little embarrassed: white First Baptist is not a shouting church. "Amen," they murmur, "amen," and become to her the people who have taken her in after the disaster that swept her old life away.

At another service, since Baptists do not believe in the spiritual efficacy of wetting the scalps of infants, Evelyn must be fully immersed in the cracked and repaired pool at the front of the church. Suitable texts are read, a sermon about baptism is preached, and Evelyn, in a white robe provided by Sister White, is asked by Brother White, who stands wet to the waist, "Do you wish to be baptized?" Upon being told that she does, he considerately holds her nose as he tips her back over his arm.

She comes up into a life of steady if inherently serial employment by Baptist families who, by hiring her, enjoy the double virtue of providing for their elderly mothers and giving a home to a rescued penitent.

47

In the leafless winter, Evelyn goes to take care of bedridden old Mrs. Rinehart and live in a small house on a side street of fountain-like pecan trees and white or gray-painted cottages, where a neighbor's rooster wakes them in the mornings. She works for room and board and a dollar a week; there are no other servants. She orders and receives deliveries from grocery and drugstore, cooks meals, and feeds and doses and changes and bathes and talks soothingly to her patient, who has suffered a stroke and is unable to speak. Evelyn reads *The Reader's Digest* aloud to Mrs. Rinehart, eliciting her approving *Uhh!* to the prospect of each article before she begins: "Marie Curie," "The German Soul," "Mrs. Wallis Simpson and Empire," and "Will China Withstand Japan?" She is unconvinced about the German soul but half admires Mrs. Wallis Simpson. Library books would be better, but Evelyn, who takes no day off, cannot check them out for fear of being unable to return them on time. She never goes beyond the yard unless relieved by a fellow Baptist to go to church or a member of her patient's family to run errands.

In the good weather, the neighbors see her out on the rickety porch swing in the evening, where she can look at the trees greening up, the daffodils blooming and drying by the fire hydrants, and the dog that lies on the middle seam of new concrete pavement. She is not unhappy: on a day in the back yard where pear trees join their foliage into a dense hide, she finds a nest of open mouths. She has a place in life again, and she knows how easy falling out of one can be.

She receives legal papers concerning *Gant vs. Gant*, consults Brother White, and stays away from the divorce hearing. She dreams it is because she burnt the peas. She is filled with uncomprehending sorrow and wakes with relief not to feel it. Mrs. Rinehart's daughter ceases to refer to her as Evelyn Gant and, in her monologue to Mrs. Rinehart, begins correcting herself, *I should say, Evelyn Kunkle.*

The Gant brothers' conviction is appealed on grounds that the instructions to the jury were faulty in not allowing for the possibility that Charles McCoy might have had only one testicle at the time of the attack. The appeal is denied and, as Evelyn learns from the *Iron Rock Standard* ("Two Ranchers' Appeal Denied"), the Gant brothers go to prison.

On the screened back porch in all weathers she loads diapers and nightgowns, sheets and towels into an electric washing machine and remembers washing in a washpot with a broomstick to punch down the ballooning fabric. She runs the wet clothes through a mangle, remembers wringing laundry by hand, and carries the heavy basket to the line. It runs along the sunny side of the small back yard, and from there she can look out between Mrs. Rinehart's house and the neighboring house to the street, although she does not need to. People who come onto that street are identifiable by sound, the clink of milk bottles, the sudden open and hard close of a sticky front door, the rattle of mailboxes, the pinging chug of the grocery truck. She hangs up clothes and linens, finding in the stoop and lift, the rhythm of *corner, clothespin, corner, clothespin,* the accessible refuge of the present.

She learns about her family only by chance or newspaper: a glimpse of bitter Al in a truck driven past on her way to Wednesday evening church; an announcement that *Mrs. Lonnie Beckendorff, neé Beatrice Kunkle, presented her husband with their first child, a girl, Marina,* Mami's name; the remark of a visitor, *I hear your baby brother hopes to go to college to study engineering.* She can only say, "He always did have that talent."

On a winter morning so cold the sheets begin to freeze as she unfurls them on the line, she looks up at an alien step from the street to see Lester Gant, Senior, in a familiar sheepskin coat now too big on him, staring down the side yard with eyes like hot holes in his face. He has lost his big heartiness and looks old.

"You ruined me," he calls from the smoke of his breath.

She bends to her basket, where her red fingers find the corner of the next white sheet. She breathes the sharp smell of disinfecting bleach, and by the time she looks up again, he is gone. *The Iron Rock Standard* reports foreclosure on his mortgaged acres, *reducing the inherited Gant property by about half.* Some people, maybe Al, would take satisfaction in that. She regrets it.

48

During the war when Evelyn works for the Westenheimers, strong farm women are hired easily at aircraft and meat packing plants in San Antonio and Ft. Worth, and some people wonder why she stays in Iron Rock. The Gants talk against her. To her own people, she might as well not exist, unless brought face to face with them in a store or at a funeral. Then one of them might say, "Hello, Evvie, how are you?" and not wait to hear. They know how she is, and how they are because of her. She thinks of leaving. She could be somebody else in another place, earn many times there what she does here. She doesn't know why she stays.

The Westenheimers feel lucky she does. She's so attentive to Mama, such an intelligent manager, such an absolutely clean housekeeper. Vivian, oldest of the daughters-in-law, who half-admired Evelyn Kunkle at school and half-thought she was too good, is intrigued by her, often goes over to the house with news, and treats her more like a friend than any of their contemporaries do. *Remember Amelia Beckendorff? She's joined the Army as a nurse!* And of course Evelyn must be proud of her little brother Sammy, two years of college and commissioned a Second Lieutenant.

What Vivian can't get over, besides Evelyn Kunkle's having finally done something wrong, is the idea of her and, *I mean, Charlie McCoy!* When Vivian hears that Charlie, who has stayed at home courted by his father since the cash settlement, has been drafted into the Army, she doesn't see anything wrong with going over to see how Evelyn Kunkle will take the news.

All the Westenheimers walk into the big four-square brick house without knocking, where, in the former living room, pale, frail Mrs. Westenheimer lies in a hospital bed staring at the ceiling. "Hello, Mama," Vivian says, and more loudly, as if it will make a difference, "we had a letter from Del, in the Marines."

Evelyn is in the kitchen, mashing a sweet potato. "I'm afraid it's not one of her good days." On good days, Mrs. Westenheimer calls her *Dorothy,* after the daughter who has moved to California for when her husband gets shore leave.

"Wes says they're building up the Army to invade Europe." It's generally known that farmers are losing their draft deferments. In the middle of this conversation, Vivian slips in *Charlie McCoy* and watches Evelyn's face.

"I suppose they'll get around to everybody, if it lasts long enough."

"They say he's hoping to be a sharpshooter."

"Seems like he'd be good at that," Evelyn says, and he might never have been more than a neighbor boy.

Vivian's husband Wes is waiting to be drafted away from the newly flourishing brewery, and Vivian is reduced to saying, "Wes says they love 'em squirrel hunters can hit a man's head at two hundred yards." Wes's point is that he is not one of them.

Vivian goes away thinking she never did believe Charlie was the reason Evelyn stays here. Maybe it's Les: if Evelyn left Iron Rock, she'd never hear anything about Les. Vivian, a fan of romance novels, has heard of a divorced couple remarrying each other after ten years.

When Les and Marvin got out of prison, although ex-cons are generally refused, strings were pulled and both men went straight into the military, Les to the Navy, Marvin to the Marines. That much, people know, but not the ironies, that Les, who wanted to die, was assigned to the relatively safe Sea-bees for his building skills, whereas Marvin, who particularly wanted not to die, has gone through the fire of Guadalcanal, New Guinea, and New Brit-ain, where he earned a Bronze Star, and is now in Australia learning to sing "Waltzing Matilda."

Even Vivian will not mention Les or Marvin to Evelyn. The closest Vivian has come to Evelyn's past is to say how, once early in the war, "Old Lester Gant came to the brewery and told Wes he ought to fire you from Mama's."

But insofar as Vivian has hoped for an opportunity to commiserate and be receptive to confidences, she is disappointed. "I'm glad Wes didn't."

"You won't believe what Lester said. He said he wanted to see you a street-walker in San Antonio."

Evelyn manages a half-laugh, in the way she can do by that time.

49

The real significance of Vivian's husband Wes Westenheimer in this story—since almost any imaginable, old-enough Baptist character could play Evelyn's wartime employer—is for something he says casually on the way to the war, from which he will return as Iron Rock's one-legged brewer. He has been drafted and ordered to report to camp and, over at his mother's house to say good-by to her whether she understands him or not, he mentions to Evelyn his regret at leaving the brewery. He has built it up since the end of Prohibition and has just moved it into the historic Westenheimer building, remodeled for the purpose. "It's so full of family history, it's like part of who I am," he says about the building, and goes off, as only readers and the omniscient author know at this point, to lose a more corporeal part of himself.

The Westenheimer building was where the old saloon had been, one of many places of communal memory for people whose white ancestors had lived around Iron Rock long enough. Westenheimers' saloon was a main setting of the Great Call-Out, the vigilante action in which the young Gant of that family's cautionary story perished corporeally and became an Iron Rock story. Although the communal memory of that action was first familial, each family telling a slightly different version of it, the family stories joined around the places that featured in everybody's. One of those places was the Westenheimer building; another was an enormous live-oak tree outside town, since uprooted by the big storm of 1905; a third was Kunkle Road.

At the time of the Great Call-Out, the newly built railroad to Iron Rock had brought strangers to town, some of doubtful purpose, others obviously gamblers who preyed on each other at the saloon and on susceptible locals. In the Gant version, one of them was the young great-uncle-to-be, but whatever his or anybody's winnings at gambling, losers who wished to continue required sources of cash. There was cash around Iron Rock during those years' harvest seasons, and some of it could be seen at Westenheimers', where men in from the country to sell a crop might drop by to spend a little before heading home. Often that fall, a farmer would be waylaid as he drove home and robbed of his season's profits by armed men with kerchiefs over their faces. Some of the robbed were also murdered, and fear and outrage spread through the county. When possible, men carrying large amounts of money hired armed guards or enlisted relatives to ride with them. The robbed who survived thought they had done so by not resisting, and some of the cool-headed noticed and remembered—or believed afterwards that they had done so—mounts, voices, facial features, pieces of clothing or tack. Afterwards, when they dared, they might sidle back to the saloon and stand as if casually outside, chewing and spitting and talking, watching as one man and another came or went on a particular animal, or they might step inside to raise a stein at the bar and listen or take quick looks around without seeming to.

After hog-killing and wurst-making, when the smoke-houses were full, *leading citizens,* as they were called in the stories—probably Westenheimers, who would've done it for the sake of the saloon's reputation—called a private meeting. They invited men who represented the established families of the county: Kunkles and Gants, of course, and McCoys by that time, Schlegels, Heimsoths, Thigpens, McAnoys, Biedermanns, Beckendorffs, all the old names. But no Gants came. The Gant story said, *They knew what it meant, and they warned and begged the young feller to get out of town, but he never heeded them.*

Evidence was introduced: *Feller in the mashed hat, tip of a gray beard sticking out from the kerchief. Feller that whistles through his teeth when he talks. I ought to recognized that filly, I sold it to his father.* A list of names was drawn up, duty volunteered for, inside or out, and a pact was sworn: nobody would ever say who had done what. A man nobody knew was hired, brought in on the train, and paid in advance.

On Christmas Eve, 1883, people quit work early and the saloon was crowded. The shutters on the deep windows, which stood open during the daytime, were closed and ordinarily latched when the lamps were lit, but *somebody*—who else but the Westenheimer running the place?—*ordered the bartender to leave them unlatched.* The inside men *by ones and twos* gathered at the bar, all armed with pistols but, under the recent circumstances, attracting no special attention by it. *Suddenly,* the Kunkles' story told, *the shutters were flung in and the windows were full of rifles,* leading the Kunkle descendants to infer that their ancestor had been an inside man.

A more detailed account of what happened inside was provided decades later to that local-historian cousin of Evelyn's, E. J. Schlegel, by an individual in the saloon whom this sudden appearance alarmed. Schlegel's book, *Old Times Around Iron Rock* (1967), includes the following account, which, he wrote there, *can be retold now without danger to anyone, as the teller has long gone penitent to his final reward.* I add from this informant's story beginning when the rifles had appeared.

I was afraid something like this might be in the making, for I had seen a quantity of rope being purchased the day before, and now feeling that they might want me, too, for what, I will not say, I stepped behind the bar and crouched among the barrels and boxes, pistol ready. The bartender must've seen me, but he did not look at me directly.

The man nobody knew came and stood just inside the door of the saloon and read out the list of names, and if a called man was in the saloon, the inside man nearest him herded him out at pistol point with his hands in the air. *When my name was called, the bartender told them, 'He was in here earlier, I think he left.' It saved my life, and I reckon he hoped it would save his.*

The outside men roped the called-out together. *In the confusion, I stepped out a suddenly vacated window, swapped horses with a man who did not know it, and got away, and I did not come back to Iron Rock for forty years.*

In the Gant story, the young Gant spoke up to defend himself, *Whatever I have done wrong, I have neither robbed nor murdered any man.*

After some consultation, one of the outside men allowed him the evidence, *Your horse was recognized.*

I have, on occasion, lost and later won back my horse on the turn of a card. He looked around at the other accused but nobody spoke. *What you reckon he expected?* was Lester Gant's line.

They were walked about a mile out of town, to the big live-oak, where a livery-stable horse waited and nooses already hung *like Christmas tree ornaments* from the big limbs. One by one, each of the accused was mounted on the horse, a noose was dropped around his neck by the man nobody knew, and the horse was whipped to a fast start.

When all the accused were dead, the bodies were laid out on the ground for anybody to claim who would, all except the young Gant's. His they tied to his mare and sent home along Kunkle Road. *Now*—this was the end of the Kunkle family story as retold by sardonic Augustus—*wasn't that a nice Christmas present from the neighbors?*

And maybe soon after Wes Westenheimer's remark Evelyn recalls some of one or the other family's account, because the next Sunday morning when she is relieved of her duties by one of the Westenheimer wives so she can go to church, she walks along the main street and turns down Westenheimer Lane so as to pass the old building, whose pinkish stone has been freshly cleaned. She can hardly be sentimental by this time in her life, and no one connected to the Gants can regard the Christmas Eve Call-Out with complacency, but she has a feeling for the old building as she passes.

It will have become a post office by the time Ernest Schlegel's book appears.

50

Vivian Westenheimer, hearing the news that Marvin Gant has been killed in the battle for Peleliu Island, "Along with about a third of the First Marine

Division," carries the excuse of summer squash from her Victory Garden to her mother-in-law's house. "It'll be in the paper," she says to Evelyn, "but I thought you'd want to know." Vivian, whose husband is in Europe, can't even tell whether Evelyn does.

"How dreadful," Evelyn says, and how sorry she is, and how terrible for the family, which reminds Vivian of nothing so much as that stainless girl, Evelyn Kunkle, who always said the right thing.

That night Evelyn wakes from a dream with the shout in her throat, *Stop!* as Marvin, but then it is Les, mysteriously with the First Marine Division, running towards a gun emplacement as photographed for a newspaper, only the lowered guns turn into pine logs that shoot down the whole line of attacking Marines. This dream is vivider than any of her volitional memories; so are the waking flashbacks when she sweats into her second-hand dress as some visitor to Mrs. Westenheimer gabbles on about whoever it was who went out to their family's fish camp or came home on leave and found his fiancée with another man.

Evelyn's dream to the contrary, Les will survive the war for another purpose in this story, though nothing like Vivian imagines. He never dreams about Evelyn. He quit wondering about her in prison, where he had to accept that both she and Charlie had betrayed him. Now assigned to underwater demolition, at the careful nerveless work of setting charges and blowing up mines, he never thinks of her at all. He tries to think only of what he is doing. Les has always liked to do a job right, and the work has possibly cured him of wanting to die: bad luck aside—the shark happens by, the shock wave hits at the wrong time—to die would be to have made a mistake. To die of bad luck, Les is content: those ragged, water-logged human parts that wash up on reefs and atolls, it's not like a fellow would know they were you. When in idle times Les thinks outside the present, it's to contemplate not the past but the unappetizing future of an ex-con.

Other men from Prince Carl County die in combat, those with any visible connection to this story including a Beckendorff, a McAnoy cousin of my mother's, and Thomas Edward Theriot, a grandson of Rebecca Thigpen Theriot. Charlie McCoy is decorated for valor in the Normandy invasion, returns to New York harbor on a troopship two years later, and dies from injuries sustained in a bar fight, but his father will claim that Charlie was killed in the war, and, after enough time has passed for people to forget they didn't hear about that at the time, Iron Rock will believe it.

51

Especially after she is bedridden, Mrs. Theriot will at times bring the conversation around to Tom Ed, *how he looked when he was a little, little boy; how he looked in his uniform when he went off to war.* At other times she recalls the son dead of influenza in Memphis, where she had not wanted him to go, or the daughter dead in childbirth in 1933, or *Mr. Theriot,* her own dead husband of forty-five years. She is not temperamentally lugubrious, speaks also of graduations and weddings and births, as well as significant passages far less public in people's lives. She is merely gifted with a taste for drama larger than her life satisfies. Surrounded by upright, church-going people of regular habits, she longs for, not scandal—that would be a sin—and certainly not anybody's misfortune, but for intense circumstances, the more absorbing and challenging of explanation the better. She has never been a reader except of selected passages in the Bible and, although hers will be one of the first households in Iron Rock to own a television, she will never be able to get very interested in distant people or characters she cannot hope to engage in conversation, or at least hear of being engaged by people she herself can then question.

In 1951, newly condemned to bed, she has been nursed by *two ninnies in succession,* both of whom she let go. Robbie is pained by her feet and cannot get her housework done for answering the upstairs bell, and a most unsatisfactory woman is staying at night, when Mrs. Theriot hears the news that Evelyn Kunkle, who has never before left a living patient, has left poor old Mrs. Hardy. Evelyn has taken refuge—those are the words that come to Mrs. Theriot—with Brother and Sister Newwhite, who have followed the Whites at First Baptist. (Brother White has died; Sister White has gone to live with a daughter in Galveston.) To Mrs. Theriot, Evelyn Kunkle seems like exactly the right kind of woman, even to the interest of her departure from Mrs. Hardy's, as Mrs. Hardy's unmarried middle-aged son visited shortly before and stayed *in the house with them.*

Interviewed, Evelyn proves to know most of the people who interest Mrs.

Theriot, aside from children born in the last fifteen years. "Why did you leave your most recent position?" Mrs. Theriot demands, and Evelyn says only, "It was unsuitable."

So there is still the interest of that, as well as the compelling question of her history: how a woman like that ever came to do what Mrs. Theriot, on a memorable winter Sunday fourteen years before, heard her confess to the congregation of First Baptist Church. Failing any answer there—because even an old lady can only get away with so much in the way of inquiry—Mrs. Theriot anticipates the simple enjoyment of knowing when she wakes up at night alone and can't get back to sleep, that the mystery of Evelyn Kunkle is asleep within call in the little dressing room adjoining the big bedroom.

None of this would Mrs. Theriot say to anybody. What she says about her new hire is that Evelyn has such good sense you don't mind having her around you all the time, *and that isn't just everybody,* an explanation calculated to squelch family objection. All the same, a daughter-in-law wonders to Mrs. Theriot's face whether children in the family ought to see such a woman there.

"You do believe in Redemption through Jesus Christ?" Mrs. Theriot demands.

"Of course, Mother Theriot. But still."

Mrs. Theriot is like her house, square-built, ruddy, and persistent. "You do believe in forgiveness of sin through Jesus Christ?"

As the daughter-in-law told later, she *practically had to recite the Creed.*

So that Mrs. Theriot could announce in triumph, "Well, if Jesus has forgiven her, I suppose Becka Theriot may do so without shame."

52

At Mrs. Theriot's big matter-of-fact house where there are other servants during the daytime, Evelyn can go out on errands for herself as she chooses— check books out of the library because she will be able to return or renew them when due—this strange freedom, after years tied to the helpless. There's no question of her using the back door, either, so when she steps down from the porch in her decent coat and unfashionable old-lady shoes, she is right there on Main Street between the new stone bank and the First Baptist Church. This afternoon, probing to be sure of the key in her purse, an admirable leather one formerly owned by Mrs. Westenheimer and given to Evelyn tactfully after her death as *a memento*, she fails at first to see Lester Gant, who is stopped at a crook in the boardwalk.

Most of this boardwalk will be replaced by concrete in a few years, which will be returned to boardwalk twenty-five years later for the tourist trade. History is as yet an unrealized asset in Iron Rock, its low, old main street buildings with their scrolled false pediments, and the boardwalk, one section of which is covered and runs along a block of stores like a front porch. Except for the hunched and hooded look of cars on the street, 1951 in Iron Rock might be any year before television antennas take over the tops of buildings.

When Evelyn looks up, there is Lester Gant, waiting again for her to notice him, now scrawny, stooped, standing bowlegged in her path. She steps firmly towards him. He looks, in his stained straw hat and khaki work clothes, like any old farmer or rancher. You have to know who he is to know he was once the largest landowner in the county and still isn't poor, however he talks. Evelyn steps off the boardwalk to pass him.

"He would've come home after the war," he bellows at her hoarsely as if at an animal, "if it hadn't been for you." Les was mustered out of the Navy at San Diego and wrote home to say so, but nobody in the family has heard from him since.

"Good afternoon," Evelyn says, and her heels knock on down the boardwalk.

A few blocks away, the boxcars and flatcars and cattle cars of a train rumble through town, the engine blowing the level crossings all in one long honk, and the sound sets her to thinking again of the passenger car that train hauls twice a week, stopping if the signal says anyone wants to get on. Lester Gant's wanting her to leave Iron Rock is no more reason to stay than to go. Rather, she thinks of leaving in terms of *really ought* and a certain fatigue with being Evelyn Kunkle, penitent. The difficulties are in weighing five dollars a week for light work in Iron Rock, all found and mostly kind company, against wages for heavy factory work in San Antonio or Ft. Worth, where she would have to pay for everything and know nobody. She tries to imagine knowing about people just what she might observe or they might tell her.

In the darkening winter afternoon Evelyn rattles her way back in through the big front door that the Theriot son who manages the drugstore has just left, and Mrs. Theriot, listening for her, is glad. She does not like to be alone too long. Now she can inquire about the temperature outdoors and the availability of particular colors of petit-point wool at Sanderson's, postponing more interesting matters to look forward to. I give Evelyn Kunkle skill in the decorative needle arts as practiced through hours of sitting at bedsides, and Mrs. Theriot, as a woman of her generation, the knowledgeable admiration of needlework, though she always says, *I never had the patience myself.*

"Show me the colors," she demands, and admires the gradual shades of red laid out on the white sheet, fingers skeins of thread and compares the new colors to the already sewn-in.

"They always sew in lighter."

When the wool is put away, Mrs. Theriot asks, "Who did you see?"

Evelyn can mention several names, but she cannot avoid Lester's, not to Mrs. Theriot. Next week somebody will sit down in the half circle of chairs around her bed and declare, *I saw Lester Gant block the sidewalk in front of your Evelyn on Saturday afternoon.*

"Lester Gant spoke to me."

And there is drama right in Mrs. Theriot's room: "What'd he say?"

"That it was my fault Les didn't come home after the war."

"Pooh. He had nothing to come home for." In Mrs. Theriot's opinion, things worth coming home for would have been family, property, or reputation. "Lester Gant is an old fool, though I never speak against family." The Thigpens are obscurely related to the Gants, *some generations back.*

53

At Mrs. Theriot's demand, although it also offends family members, Evelyn shares meals with her, sitting next to the bed and eating off a card table. Give them a winter supper of soup and cornbread Robbie has left for them, and Mrs. Theriot asks, "Do yeh miss the pines?"

As much as to ask, does she miss the lives she formerly led. "Sometimes the silence in town wakes me at night."

But Evelyn's evasion of polite prying is only the opportunity for Mrs. Theriot to reminisce, with the evening closed in around them, about her own nine-teenth-century youth as a daughter of privilege, when the drugstore—and Negro field labor, but she does not think of that—had for a time subsidized Daddy Thigpen's dream of becoming a cotton planter. "And you know where that got him, but it was grand while it lasted." The tall frame house, long since pulled down, that rose starkly out of fields now sold; her sixteenth birthday party, when Daddy rented a tent, barbecued two hogs, and invited the county; the unheard-of automobile trip he and her mother and a couple of brothers made when they were old, to California over dirt roads in a Model-T, for utter glee at having lived to a time when that could be done.

"I wanted so badly to go." Mrs. Theriot was the mother of many children by then. "If I had been invited, I would've left them all for it."

Every night before the two women go to bed, they take turns reading out loud from the Bible: at Evelyn's suggestion they are reading it straight through, front to back, as neither of them has ever done. They discover how much more of it there is than the familiar passages from church. Sometimes Mrs. Theriot closes the Book saying, *And if you can make head or tail of that, you're smarter than this old woman,* though she has no doubt it is the literal Word of God. One of her many hopes in the reading is that some passage may inspire Evelyn to mention her own sin.

Other times, when Mrs. Theriot sees an inoffensive opportunity, she tries to nudge Evelyn to do that. As, for instance, deep in the night when she herself has to use the bedpan and rings the brass hand-bell that belonged to a frontier cousin schoolteacher, and when Evelyn has lifted her onto the bedpan—no easy task—asks her, "D'yeh ever get to thinking about things at night?"

Evelyn, still young-looking with her graying braids hanging over her shoulders, wearing one of the long, hand-smocked nightgowns she makes for herself, says, "Sometimes I ponder the words we've read."

Another of those entirely proper, unsatisfying answers, but then Mrs. Theriot can speak of her own sorrows, how she was still angry at her son Tom when he died, how the family could not even bring young Tom Ed's body home from a place in Europe called Anzio.

54

Working at Mrs. Theriot's Evelyn is reintroduced to white Iron Rock society, of which the part able to have an opinion is divided about her. Iron Rock society comprises not only the living but several generations of dead, and these, although incapable of opinion, are not so dead as they would be in some places.

At times, say when Mrs. Theriot's banker, lawyer, or the son who manages Thigpen and Theriot calls on her, Evelyn is excused to her own freedom and, when she doesn't go out, sits in the parlor where the drawn green shades in the daytime are rimmed with sun. She reads if she has a library book; the glass-fronted bookcases in the parlor run to pious tomes, *The Way of Obedience,* and crumbling adventure novels, *You Were There With Quantrill's Raiders.* Without a book, she might pick up one of the albums of fading photographs that lie on the parlor tables and page through the citizens posed on the steps of churches and schools in groups identified in white ink on the black pages: "Class of 1925," "Woodmen of the World," "Old Settler's Reunion." In her own era, she can identify many of them, the faces of Kunkles and Schlegels like amputated limbs stirring sensation in her. She recognizes again her Papi and Uncle Willi, with other men in front of the *Verein;* her Aunt and Uncle Gainer over the top of a grand piano, posed as if to play duets. Regarding the older generations, Evelyn is sometimes moved to carry a crumbling album upstairs, where there seems scarcely a visage Mrs. Theriot cannot identify: the Kunkle grandfather as a shiny-faced young man—*Opa, my Opa!*—on a log front porch with an unrelated man in an umbrella-sized palm-leaf hat.

"And do you know who that is? That is old Morse Hardy, who owned a big farm adjoining Daddy Thigpen's and whose daughter-in-law would be Florence Hardy, mother of that young Mr. Hardy whom," Mrs. Theriot says coyly, "you know, I believe, to your regret?"

People might regard Mrs. Theriot as impertinent if she were poorer or less well connected; Evelyn, inured to curious questions, rather admires her. "I have nothing to regret concerning Mr. Hardy."

55

After Mrs. Theriot gets the television, in a bulky cabinet Josiah sets up on a stout table where she can see it with her glasses on, she and Evelyn watch "I Love Lucy," where Lucy Ricardo is pregnant but in 1952 the word cannot be spoken. Lucy must be " . . .expecting?" as Ethel Mertz asks at the end of a long routine of comic misunderstandings, and Lucy, round-eyed, nods. The proprieties of showing this condition on television will be much discussed around Mrs. Theriot's bed, where Mrs. Theriot will repeat for her various audiences, "I was neither pregnant nor expecting. I was in a delicate condition, which was not mentioned even when it could be seen a block away."

But even the first time she says that, when she and Evelyn are watching the show, Lucy and Ethel do not stop to say so much as, *You're kidding*, an instance of what Mrs. Theriot has against television.

Afterwards, watching Evelyn's face, she says, "Women have done the most extraordinary things trying to get pregnant."

But there is no sign. Evelyn says, "I used to hear all the old superstitions. Watch for the full moon." At least she will allude to certain aspects of her past, in a general way.

"Stick a knife in the mattress for a boy." They laugh a little, in the shadows of Mrs. Theriot's daughter dead in first childbirth, Evelyn's mother worn out by nine of them. "They used to say it took two women to have a big family, one to bear them, one to raise them."

"I raised half of one."

"They blamed a woman if she didn't get pregnant."

"I felt like I'd already had my family by the time I was grown."

"And sometimes they blamed her if she did. Montgomery Parsons, long before you would've known anything about it, hit his pregnant wife over the belly with the dasher to a butter churn, and not even Monte Parsons could have doubted that child was his."

In Evelyn's sound of conventional regret, no self-consciousness at all.

"One of those men jealous of his own children," Mrs. Theriot explains absently, thinking about whether she can get any more out of this subject. "Are you old enough to remember Homecoming of 1919?"

"The dead woman in the brush arbor."

"Who might've done nothing worse than marry the wrong man, but some people will always assume the worst about a woman. . .."

This truth fails to fetch so much as a commiserating sigh from Evelyn, of whom, granting her admirable reticence, Mrs. Theriot inclines to think she can scarcely have had the most obvious likely motive.

"My mother," Evelyn says, "when she was dying, thought that unfortunate woman had been one of a family of girls called Schachner. Did you know any Schachners?"

56

The big refrigerated air conditioner installed in Mrs. Theriot's bedroom sticks out a window on the alley between her house and First Baptist, and the congregation can hear it switching on during quiet moments. They themselves sit under hypnotic ceiling fans, subject to re-decide at any moment whether it's better to sit perfectly still in the faint motion of hot air or to heat themselves up that bit more by fanning themselves with the church bulletin.

Other people have heard of Mrs. Theriot's refrigerated air conditioner, and one afternoon Lester Gant, sweating as he leaves Kunkle Feed and Seed—operated in this generation by a Henderson—hears the famous unit switch on from across the street. Lester has known Becka Theriot since he was a boy and she was a young matron in extravagant hats, and the Theriots had looked down on the Gants as people with no cash, and the Gants had looked down on the Thigpens and Theriots as people with nothing but. He ambles across the street in a stiff-legged way more about bad knees than swagger, climbs the door step of Becka Theriot's big house, and lets the big brass knocker fall several times.

Waiting, he feels again the shrinkage of his patrimony, his failure to pass on to his sons the land he had restored for them. The door is opened and he stands face to face with Evelyn Kunkle, who looks flustered, as well she might.

"I want to talk to Becka Theriot."

"I don't know if she's receiving visitors."

"You mean me. Well, go find out."

Although reluctant to let him into the gleaming, food-scented hallway,

Evelyn cannot leave a familiar white man waiting on the stoop. He comes in removing his hat, spreading the odors of sweat and cow manure.

In the frigid bedroom, Mrs. Theriot says stoutly, "Show him up. And you may be excused to the parlor until he has gone. Tell Robbie to be prepared to show him out." Mrs. Theriot, ordinarily too warm, buttons her nylon bed-jacket over her copious breasts.

Lester comes in civil, hearty, the reminiscence of an earlier self. "Afternoon, Becka. Haven't seen you since you foundered and took to your bed."

"Isn't this something? Beats having them shoot me." She does not invite him to sit down. "How you doing these days, Lester?"

"You know how I'm doing, I lost two sons to the war." That's what Lester says ever since he quit saying Les would be home *when he gets the war out of his system.*

Mrs. Theriot looks straight through Lester Gant. "I lost a grandson. He'd be twenty-seven this summer."

"And you've probably got twenty of them."

"Sixteen, and six greats, and you and I both know it doesn't make a particle of difference about the ones you've lost. Ones you still have doing well?"

"No Gants are doing well." That's another thing Lester Gant says, and even a mention of the price of beef, with wartime controls removed and drought to the north and west, can't jolt him into any appearance of satisfaction.

"I lost half my land to that woman you got opening the door for you. I'm here to advise you to get rid of her, she's a bad lot."

"Lester, I'd thank you for your good intentions, if I believed you had any."

"My intentions are to see her as a streetwalker in San Antone, where she belongs."

"The judgment of those intentions"—Mrs. Theriot purses her lips—"I'll leave to the good God Who made both of you. What I want to know is what fits you to give me advice about a woman I employ?"

"You're treating a whore like a decent woman."

"Pooh. You don't know anything about whores or decent women either. You lucked into a good wife, and God bless her. Give her my regards." Mrs. Theriot reaches for the brass school bell.

Robbie, a big woman, opens the door so soon she must've been waiting at the top of the stairs. "Robbie, show Mr. Gant out."

"Sir," Robbie says with a precise little bow of the head that means, *You're a white man but just you try to do anything to me.*

"Come back and see me in a better state of mind, Lester, before we both die." When he is gone, Mrs. Theriot blows out her lips and shakes her head until her cheeks wobble.

She replays this conversation for Evelyn, word for word, except for *whore*, which Mrs. Theriot renders as, *well-I-won't-say-it.*

"Vivian Westenheimer told me he said the same thing to Wes."

"Did you know Lester Gant's first love was not Tessa Heimsoth but Lila Beckendorff, when she was still Lila McAnoy?" Lila is a member of Mrs. Theriot's card-playing group, a somewhat younger replacement for a dead older one. She is also a great aunt of Beatrice Kunkle Beckendorff's husband.

"They were sixteen and thought too young to marry—though I was married at seventeen—and people believed he was waiting for her, but she got engaged to Deet Beckendorff and married him instead."

Mrs. Theriot may have said this for any of several reasons, but she alludes to it again the next day, when her niece Mrs. McAnoy, who never so much as acknowledges Evelyn's presence, comes to visit. "Do you remember," Mrs. Theriot asks Mrs. McAnoy, "when Lester Gant was sparking Lila?"

"Why, Auntie, what made you think of that?"

Evelyn sits by the bed, eyes on the linen crochet work she changes to from long habit in the summer, although she could go on doing wool petit-point in Mrs. Theriot's air conditioning. This project, almost finished, is an old-fashioned doily: a plain central circle frilling out into arcs and flowers, and, from the tips of its dangling petals, single threads of fringe. Now Mrs. Theriot is telling how Lester Gant paid "a brief call on me yesterday," but Evelyn is unconcerned: Mrs. Theriot will not mention her to Mrs. Mack. "He poor-mouthed awhile, and we remembered our war dead."

Evelyn is fixed, rather, on the strangeness of mind, that hers has just joined Mrs. McAnoy's amid the tangled halo of their separate knowledge of Lester Gant, lighting like two flies on his early courtship of her sister, although Evelyn is certain Mrs. Mack would prefer to be joined by Evelyn Kunkle in nothing. But Mrs. Mack cannot control this union of mind on memory. Certainly not the plain central public memories like the Call-Out that anyone local has a version of somebody's telling about; but also not the particular scrolls and scallops and flowers of less public memory around them, such as Lester Gant's rejection by his first love. Whether anybody likes it, there is a common mind among people who have lived around Iron Rock for long, thinning to points towards its edge and tying off in single fringes, each belonging to only one person. Evelyn tries to imagine young Lila McAnoy crying when she could not marry young Lester—how hard to imagine her young, at all!—and refuses even to try to imagine him as Lila might remember him, remembers instead an aging man with hot holes in his face, spying down a frigid alley from the smoke of his breath.

57

One cold evening in 1953, the only telephone at Mrs. Theriot's, which still hangs downstairs on the hallway wall, rings too late. Having one on her bedside table would make more sense, but she prefers to have the telephone answered for her. Paul Theriot, who manages Thigpen and Theriot, instructs Evelyn to, "Tell Mama everything's all right, only I have to talk to her tonight. Privately." In the hallway, dark wood gleams in the light from the bedroom.

"Probably caught one of them stealing from the till," Mrs. Theriot remarks; everybody who works there is a close relative.

In the upper and lower hallways Evelyn turns on a dazzle of electric light, then, in the brown parlor where she will sit, a glass-shaded lamp. Paul Theriot, a middle-aged man wearing a dress topcoat and rimless glasses, rings the bell politely but as Evelyn makes to show him upstairs says, "No need." He does not look at her, his refusal different from Mrs. McAnoy's and entirely about him: all the Theriot sons are shy, *cowed by their mother,* people say.

Evelyn has finished her library book, and failed to bring her petit-point. She takes down *You Were There With Quantrill's Raiders* and turns the pages, from which she would not learn if she didn't already know that they were murderers and stock thieves whom Confederate authorities tried to use against Unionists in Texas and found themselves used by, instead, to license crime.

When Paul descends the stairway and she goes to let him out, he looks at her directly with such compassion she understands that his visit has something to do with her. She locks the door, climbs the stairs, turns out the lights in lower then upper hallway.

"Come sit by me, my dear," Mrs. Theriot says kindly, and Evelyn fears who. "I'm afraid it's your brother Sam."

Her beloved Sammy, of whom she knows only that he came home from the war, finished his degree, and settled in Ft. Worth as an engineer; that he married in the Methodist church, and, at least once, sang a tenor solo there. Now she hears as if from a distance the incomplete story of a West Texas hunting accident while crossing a fence.

"They think he, or one of the other men, must've propped a shotgun against the fence." Mrs. Theriot does not know that this younger brother was Evelyn's more than any of them.

"I am so dreadfully sorry to have to tell you he has passed on." She suppresses even the thought of Paulie's, *It blew his head off.*

Evelyn takes it quietly, as she takes everything, though in the moment it seems to her as if every fear for children must come true in the end.

She does not sleep that night, will not even lie down, spends the night in the chair next to Mrs. Theriot's bed, and is haggard the next day. For the first time in her employment at Mrs. Theriot's, she will not obey: Mrs. Theriot keeps telling her to lie down and take a nap. She falls heavily asleep that night and awakens screeching, "Stop!" from a dream she will not remember.

"Come here, my dear, I need you," Mrs. Theriot calls repeatedly, until Evelyn stumbles to sit in the chair by the bed, where Mrs. Theriot's hard old claw grips her hand.

"I'm so sorry to wake you."

"You know I don't sleep. Get yourself a blanket out of the closet," Mrs. Theriot orders, and they sit in silence, Mrs. Theriot clutching Evelyn by the hand until she goes to sleep in the chair.

All spring and summer, she will have these episodes. News of the distant death will get around, she will receive condolences from fellow Baptists and the more sympathetic of Mrs. Theriot's family and friends, and she will accept them politely and seem quite normal. So that when anybody asks while she is out of the room, *How is she?* Mrs. Theriot can say, *Oh, about as well as can be expected,* and that's the end of it. She does not want to be told to get rid of a nurse who needs nursing. Nobody has needed Mrs. Theriot in the middle of the night for a long time.

Too, although she would not wish suffering on anybody, let alone dear Evelyn, there is the opportunity for secret indignation: shame on the Kunkles for not coming to share their mourning with their many-years' penitent and irreproachable sister. They used to be such high-minded people. Mrs. Theriot holds this opinion because the Kunkle ancestor was among those who wanted nothing to do with slavery, unlike the Thigpens, who granted it was wrong but—so many wrong things being carried on in the ordinary way of the world—needed a War and an Emancipation to make them give it up.

All spring and summer Evelyn wakes shouting from dreams she goes on saying she doesn't remember after she does: the cattle truck hurtling into the clearing towards a baby she knows is Sammy; the home where she arrives too late, only to see a strange boy leap off the porch and run away through the pines; the rock house where she lived as a bride, with a high window she has never noticed before and in it the watery, disapproving face of a young man she ought to know and doesn't.

58

After school starts again in the fall Mrs. Richard Henderson can make her second surreptitious visit to her sister in seventeen years. She has taken advantage of a ladies' event at the Lutheran church to walk down the alley behind it, enter Mrs. Theriot's back yard by a wooden gate next to the garage, and tell Robbie at the back door, "Just say Liesel, for a minute." Robbie, who doesn't know her, admits her as a well-dressed white woman with a right-sounding name.

Poor Liesel has been made a coward by her marriage to a man who is *deeply disappointed* if any small thing within her assigned purview falls short of his wishes. Waiting in the big, old-fashioned kitchen, she imagines what he would say about her *slipping into Mrs. Theriot's big house by the back door. If you had only gone to the front door!* But it's not about doors. If Liesel had gone to Mrs. Theriot's by the front door, he would be *deeply disappointed* that she has gone at all, just now. *Any other time,* he would plead, which is to say that Sammy has been killed at an inconvenient time: Richard is running for County Commissioner.

Evelyn, already in tears, bursts down the stairs and into the kitchen, and the sisters embrace over their losses, all of them: "Our darling Sammy," "I know, I know."

"I would've come sooner," Liesel says, but not why she didn't. She won't sit down, can only stay for a moment.

Time for a few questions: hers, "Are you treated well?"; half an apology, "I've been sorry so many times that I. . .," Evelyn's, "Did you go to the funeral?" "Do they have children?"

No time for the questions impossible anyway: *Did Sammy hate me? Is it Richard that's changed you so?*

The doorbell rings, Robbie's heavy tread from the dining room shakes the floor, and there is no time, after so long. Never mind that Evelyn might shut the kitchen door and hope for Mrs. Theriot's discretion: Liesel is like the chance-met on a railway platform; Evelyn the emigrant too briefly returned when the train comes in. They move apart, blowing kisses, Liesel to emerge from the back door into the difficult transition between love and the public, Evelyn to reach the upper hallway as Robbie admits visitors below.

"Please don't mention to anybody that I had a visitor. I can't say who it was."

Mrs. Theriot can guess what category of who. "Sit down and compose yourself, my dear." At least one of them had the decency.

59

Evelyn does not have the dreams anymore after that, and one day when Mrs. Theriot has awakened from a nap and Evelyn is sitting by the bed—in the fall, still—crocheting, she says "When Sammy was deciding to stay on at the old house, he said to me how memory attaches to places."

"I would've said to people." But Mrs. Theriot can, indeed, look over at the highboy and see her young husband Ed Theriot stretching his neck up as he fastens a collar stud such as men haven't worn these fifty-odd years.

Having gotten to one of the many somewheres in the progress of grief, Evelyn wants to talk about Sammy's places. "It's like each place has a spark of his mind, so if you know he remembered a place, you know a spark of him is still there, and one of you can be, too."

Mrs. Theriot knows the dead are in heaven—or the other place—but she wouldn't deny Evelyn any little comforting. "You may have Josiah and the car, if one day you wish to go out to your old home place." To Mrs. Theriot it seems impractical: one of the brothers still lives out there, and she has heard they all regard Evelyn as dead.

"'We think we remember places,'" Evelyn quotes and could not say where from, "'but they remember us.'"

60

The Iron Rock Standard, whose weekly edition is delivered to Mrs. Theriot's house on Fridays just before noon, has been reprinting the names of the war dead of Prince Carl County in the edition nearest the tenth anniversary of their deaths. But the small headline, "We Remember," at the bottom of the first page, does not appear every week: the war dead of the county total only about sixty. In her careful economy of pleasures, Mrs. Theriot saves the paper to read after dinner, and when she opens it looks first, while Evelyn is still there, for the small headline. If it appears, she reads out the name and recalls the people she has known of that family, or of their name, or, if she has never known people of that name, anybody she has known of similar name. The week of the anniversary of D-Day, when Evelyn and Mrs. Theriot are sitting over the dinner dishes, she reads out, "Charles McCoy. Omaha Beach, June 6, 1944."

As neither of them knows, Charlie McCoy died in a February, and the tenth anniversary of his death is a year and a half away, but *The Iron Rock Standard* accepts his father's memory of him as killed in the Normandy invasion. Privately Mrs. Theriot recalls Charlie McCoy as a resentful, disreputable-looking young man, although she sees now, from film advertisements featuring James Dean, or that Marlon what's-his-name, how that might have been the attraction—if in fact there was one.

She recalls for Evelyn that Charles McCoy's mother was Inge Biedermann, and what a beautiful garden she had; how, for years and years, Mrs. McCoy's was the place to beg a few branches or bouquets for graduations, recitals, weddings, funerals. "Before we had a florist in Iron Rock."

Evelyn's "I remember" gives permission, as Evelyn realizes, for whatever inquisitive question Mrs. Theriot is leading up to. "I always liked Mrs. McCoy."

"Poor Charlie McCoy. Poor all the young men, hardly alive before they were dead." Mrs. Theriot lays the paper aside. "Didja love him?"

As it is only Mrs. Theriot, easy enough to answer, "Not at all."

"I didn't think so!" How she loves to be right.

"Did ye. . .," Mrs. Theriot pronounces this word as of something foreign to both of them, "lust for him?"

"Not at all." Evelyn begins to load dishes onto the bamboo tray.

"I didn't think so. Then how in the world did you ever manage to break the seventh commandment with him?"

"I'll just carry these downstairs, ma'am," Evelyn says, the form of address unusual for her, "so Robbie can clean up and get out of the kitchen."

Thus reminded not to take advantage of the help, Mrs. Theriot lays a tip-bent arthritic finger alongside her thick nose and fixes Evelyn Kunkle with a sympathetic gaze. *Another time, my dear.*

As Mrs. Theriot will go to sleep reading the paper, Evelyn can stay downstairs until she does, and that will be the end of it for now. The vision of Charlie McCoy comes back to her from inside the shack, the gleam of the knife blade under the hook, but it doesn't seem to matter much, possibly because something so much worse has happened since.

She has planned to linger in the kitchen, but Robbie and Josiah, fellow workers of forty years, are still sitting over their own dinner at the kitchen table. In that way of refusing to acknowledge her that so oddly resembles Mrs. McAnoy's, they acknowledge her whiteness—"Miss Evelyn."

Since she avoids the parlor except when formally released by Mrs. Theriot, she crosses the hall into a dining room half-stripped of chairs for the arc around Mrs. Theriot's bed. A side window looks out onto a strip of dry, tree-grown yard and a high wooden fence along the property line, and she dares to visit the memory of that distant summer: Charlie McCoy's long siege of her—to what purpose?—when he didn't like her any better than she liked him. That boneheaded unwillingness of Les Gant's to believe and protect her, as if he saw something completely different from what she did. Her exhaustion and exasperation at Charlie's desire to put that thing into her, an act that seems now even more disproportionately slight. In the yard outside the window, black-barked saplings have grown up around an enormous, much pruned but still diseased-looking oak tree, which will have to be cut down. Evelyn thinks of a time when those saplings will have spread out towards their own maturity: Mrs. Theriot will have passed on, and this house will be a Sunday school building, as she has willed it to the church to be.

How kind she has been, and how dearly she wants to know what Evelyn herself has just now been remembering, *How I ever did that with Charlie McCoy.*

Once in a store on the main street, which has an old stamped tin ceiling, Evelyn heard a man's lowered voice say, "McCoy's fish camp," from which she supposes that's what it's called now. Maybe Old Man McCoy has closed the road, put up a fence. Kunkles and Gants would, in any case, have stopped going there. Whatever the place is called, she herself will always be linked to it, like the hanged young Gant to the road his body was sent home along, or the woman whipped to death at the cemetery. As long as anybody peoples those places in stories, she will be the adulterous wife on whose account a man was castrated at McCoy's fish camp.

With her long training in acceptance, she can accept that. And yet, aware of owning no more that she can fit into a suitcase—though, really, it's enough—she has a feeling for everything she has lost to this local immortality. Not that she dwells on her losses, only that she knows them lost to that moment in the rotten-smelling shack, *Let him.* Surely, she thinks, she may withhold this scrap from the memory of any other person.

Perhaps she seeks to do so partly to remain a person in her own world, understanding that she has already become a character in the local story. Although I have long since dramatized her secret here in the service of a worked world of the imagination, I give her to withhold it from any person she knows. Also, in a small gesture acknowledging the different priorities of life from those of art, to withhold, from an old woman who wants to know, what Mrs. Hardy's son did or said that occasioned Evelyn's departure from his employ.

61

It is dark outside now in a Southwestern city where I'm staying for a short while, and, leaving my document on the screen, I get up from my keyboard and go out. I drive to the thinning edge of town, park on an unpaved lot, and go into a bar I have noticed earlier and never been in. I love places where nobody knows me and I know nobody, and they talk.

A large work of taxidermy, parts of which once belonged to a palomino horse, stands just inside the doorway with, chained and padlocked to it, a silver-mounted saddle. A small engraved plaque on it claims for its origin, "Calf-Roping Championship, Calgary Stampede, 1947." As I slide onto a stool at one end of the bar, a jukebox I will later discover to be packed with the songs of World War Two is playing, "I'll Be Seeing You."

A man sitting at the middle of the bar conducts a laconic conversation with an old straw-hatted cowboy sitting at the other end, his knotty workingman's hand loosely around a beer bottle. "That's right," he says, "they didn't call 'em SEALs 'til after that."

Though I saw the old man as a cowboy at first, follow-up glances discover what might be the habit of greater responsibility in him or the confidence of somewhat greater resources. We are beyond the suburbs of Tucson, Albuquerque, Amarillo, the kind of city Les Gant might pass through or live near in pursuit of his determination to stay away from Iron Rock.

"Yeah," he says, "they'd send us out into the bay at night in nothing but bathing suits and diving gear to disable 'em floating mines." He knocks back the rest of his beer—an empty shot glass sits in front of him—and orders the same again.

"You'd be down there trying not to hold your breath, and you'd hear one go off and be sorry for the guy that got it, but you'd have to hope it wasn't too close. 'Cause it was like chumming for sharks."

Maybe he's managed a ranch and run a few cattle of his own on somebody else's land. Maybe he's trucking a few animals to market and stopped off at the frankly plywood motel across the highway. Whoever he works for respects him, maybe wonders about him but already knows not to ask. His known life history begins, *When I got out of the Navy after the war.* He never tells anybody he spent five years in prison before it; maybe the way he has settled down into thinking about it is, *I cut a man bad in a fight*. He has no close friends, nor wants any, and he certainly never married again: Les is the kind of man for whom the failure of one love is final. But whatever he's had in the way of a life, it's been *more than Marvin*, he thinks, the times he gets to weighing it up.

I'm not set on this identification. Maybe the sun-wrinkled stranger is some other old man who will seem to tell the most interesting stories of his life without doing so—as if he would or could. All the same, I order my small fiery luxury and settle myself to listen to what Les Gant might tell, hoping for bits to lay next to others like a painter of a bygone age who has laid out some mythic story by surrounding the enactment of a central drama with what appear at first to be only bits of scenery. Closer look discovers in them small enactments of other dramas belonging to the same story so that it becomes a design pigmented in space, the thickness of an idea told in time spread to a layer on canvas.

About the author

Elizabeth Harris is a native Texan who grew up in Fort Worth and in Pittsburgh, Pennsylvania. She won the John Simmons Prize, awarded by University of Iowa Press, for her first book, *The Ant Generator*, a collection of stories praised for their "sense of wonder and comedy" and "acid-etched existentialism." Those and uncollected stories appeared in *Antioch Review, Epoch, Chicago Review, North American Review, Shenandoah*, and other magazines, and have been anthologized in *New Stories from the South, Best of Wind, The Iowa Award*, and *Literary Austin*. She was a runner up in a previous Gival Press contest with *The Look Thief*, a contemporary novel; and in a Faulkner Pirate's Alley competition for an earlier novel. She taught fiction writing and modern literature for a number of years at the University of Texas in Austin, where she and her husband live.

Acknowledgments

This is a work of fiction. I am indebted to many accounts of life in Central Texas and the South, including oral stories of my own family and the local histories and newspapers of several Texas towns, but no event or character is intended as a representation or interpretation of an actual place, event, or person. I am extraordinarily grateful for Bertram Wyatt-Brown's *Southern Honor: Ethics and Behavior in the Old South* (Oxford University Press, 1982), which illuminated several characters and their relations for me. I thank the Michener Center for Writers at the University of Texas for a summer research fellowship and Cassandra Clarke for library research. Warmest thanks also to my earliest readers, Wick, Dunya, Tom, Martha, Tracy, and Sandra.

Books from Gival Press—Fiction & Nonfiction

Maximus in Catland by David Garrett Izzo

Middlebrow Annoyances: American Drama in the 21st Century by Myles Weber

The Pleasuring of Men by Clifford H. Browder

Riverton Noir by Perry Glasser

Second Acts by Tim W. Brown

Secret Memories / Recuerdos secretos by Carlos Rubio

Show Up, Look Good by Mark Wisniewski

The Smoke Week: Sept. 11-21. 2001 by Ellis Avery

The Spanish Teacher by Barbara de la Cuesta

That Demon Life by Lowell Mick White

Tina Springs into Summer / Tina se lanza al verano by Teresa Bevin

The Tomb on the Periphery by John Domini

Twelve Rivers of the Body by Elizabeth Oness

For a complete list of Gival Press titles, visit: *www.givalpress.com*. Books are available from Ingram, Follett, Brodart, your favorite bookstore, the Internet, or from Gival Press.

Gival Press, LLC
PO Box 3812Arlington, VA 22203
givalpress@yahoo.com
703.351.0079